Southern Lights

Cas Dunlap

Also by Cas Dunlap
It's News To Us
Beach Breezes
The Casa Linda Chronicles: Short Stories and Stuff
The Process
Celestial Blues
Flock 'Em!

Copyright © 1998 by Cas Dunlap
All rights reserved
First Edition 1998
Second Printing 1998
Third Printing 2006

ACKNOWLEDGMENT
Thank you to Hugh Armstrong for permission to use his creation *Summer* as cover art for *Southern Lights*.

The characters and events in this book are fictitious. Any similarity to real persons, living or dead, is coincidental and is not intended by the author.

Anegada Press
Pensacola Beach, Florida

Printed in the United States of America
Bodree Printing, Pensacola, Florida

Library of Congress Control Number 2006901957

ISBN 0-9670420-0-3

*F*oreword
...from the author

What you are about to read is a "beach book." It won't cause Larry McMurtry to be looking over his shoulder, and at the end you won't be wondering what it really meant. It's a fun book that unfolds in a fun place and that I had fun writing.

Ideally, you're in Pensacola Beach for a long weekend, and you picked up the book in one of the island shops because it looked like you could finish it while you were here and leave it in the motel room. I say "ideally" because that's the kind of book it is. You can read it all weekend long, if you limit your reading to the time when you're tanning your back, or you can wolf it all down in one day under the umbrella. It's best when read sprawled out on a beach chair on the sugar-white sand facing the Gulf of Mexico with an ice cold beer within easy reach.

Hope you enjoy reading it as much as I enjoyed writing it.

Southern Lights

Chapter *I*

Peg Leg Pete's is a beach bar and oyster house seated along the Gulf of Mexico on Pensacola Beach. Its major claims to fame are that, first and foremost, it looks like a beach bar, the kind you think of when Jimmy Buffett sings about the beach. It doesn't hurt its attraction that it has several kinds of good beer on tap, great oysters on the half-shell, and an outdoor volleyball court for the deckside viewing pleasure of its patrons.

This night, as fugitives from a day on the beach cooled their sunburned bodies with ice cold beer, and as the last light of day disappeared, the crowd was treated to a rare vision of the "Southern Lights."

"Kaboom!" was the sound that first got the deck crowd's attention, followed by a shock wave that spilled beer and jostled the stacks of oysters.

The first reaction was that another jet from the Naval Air Station had broken the sound barrier while doing an overly fast fly-by. This was a definite no-no by long agreement between the Navy and the local residents and merchants. On closer investigation, though, the brilliant glow from the beach proclaimed that something more than a broken sound barrier was responsible for the hubbub. In that mindset, the first thought was that, for some reason, an airplane had actually crashed on the beach.

"Help! Call 911. Call an ambulance," came the hysterical cries from the direction of what was now clearly a large bonfire.

Reacting in the fine tradition of witnesses everywhere, one girl was knocked off Peg Leg's deck onto the volleyball court and another reveler broke his foot racing harem-skarem toward the beach to get a closer look at whatever death and destruction there was to see. What they discovered, after dodging through the lengthening line of gawking motorists on Fort Pickens Road, was a fiercely blazing "beach box" and two smoldering bodies, apparently one of each sex, sprawled in the renowned sugar-white sand.

The consensus among the onlookers in the know was that the beach box – the overnight storage for rental umbrellas, chairs, kayaks, and other beach paraphernalia – had been torched, and the two who were injured were either the "perps" who weren't quite quick enough, or strolling innocents who just happened to be in the wrong place at the wrong time. Of course, other theories were advanced concerning errant Navy missiles, drug deals gone bad, and alien invasion, but those seemed less likely, even after a lot of cold beer from Peg Leg's.

In fairly short order, the Escambia County Sheriff's Department, accompanied by an M.I.C.U., arrived and, as the fire dwindled of its own accord, the crowd began wandering off for further discussion of the evening's big event, or to wherever they'd been destined in the first place. Only the truly dedicated remained to watch the paramedics inter the scorched victims into body bags.

*****

Sheriff Slidell Goodbee was not a happy man. Five hours previous, he had been headed for the Angus, anticipating a bottle of wine, a good meal of maybe snapper throats, and the charms of Daphne Fairhope. Now he sat in the dimly lit office of the Escambia County Coroner listening to Dr. Ling explain that the cause of death of the two bodies recovered earlier on Pensacola Beach had been the result of burning. Dr. Ling deduced that both had been knocked to the ground by the shock wave of an explosion, and shortly thereafter ignited by the following fireball. Mercifully, both were probably rendered unconscious by the initial impact of the shock wave.

Slidell had no reason to doubt anything Ling said in a professional capacity, and assumed that if Ling said it, it was

County, or the state for that matter, knew better than to bad mouth the Fairhopes, even indirectly.

The fact of the matter was that Slidell had every intention of "making an honest woman" of Daphne. He just hadn't had the time, what with his career and all. Aside from lawing, there was nowhere Slidell would rather be than with Daphne. In any case, it had all worked out. Farley lost, but by a very slim margin. Thereafter, Slidell did such a creditable job that no one ever thought about running against him. That, plus now he was an incumbent with incredible influence.

However, none of those things, especially failing to show up at the Angus to meet Daphne, made Slidell any happier after leaving the office of Joe Don Ling and arriving at his own desk well past midnight. Learning that the two people had burned to death was like learning that the sand on the beach was white. The question was, what were they doing out there, and why had the beach box exploded in flames?

Slidell hoped forensics would come up with something on the beach box. In the meantime, he was sorting through the remains of the clothing that had been removed by the coroner's people or recovered from the area around the bodies. About the only thing worth anything was the wallet found in the male's clothing. It had survived the burning pretty well. The female apparently wasn't carrying a purse. Either that or it had been blown into the gulf, or one of the local beach thieves had captured it before his deputies arrived.

The name on the driver's license was Raymond Thomas Adkins, a thirty-five-year-old white male who was licensed to drive in Texas and lived at an address in Dallas that had no meaning to Slidell. Joe Don had found no identifying scars or tattoos, but those kinds of identifying marks might have been removed by the burning. No wedding rings were found. They could have been blown off. Things like that happened sometimes.

Not much to go on, Slidell knew. Tomorrow he'd contact the Dallas County Sheriff's Office and try to learn more. Maybe he'd be better off calling the Dallas Police Department, but he'd get better treatment from a fellow sheriff – probably. Anyway, it wouldn't hurt to try the sheriff first. If that didn't work out, maybe one of his deputies knew someone at Dallas PD. At any rate, it was too late to be calling people now. Besides, it'd keep 'til the morning.

The only other thing was to contact the owner of the beach box, who might be able to shed some light on what happened and why. Although the owner probably already knew through the beach grapevine, procedure dictated that Slidell notify the owner. That seemed fair. The last arriving report from one of his deputies indicated that the beach box owner was Robert Ernest Brown.

Chapter II

Robert Ernest "Honest Ernest" Brown had become a local fixture since his arrival at Pensacola Beach three years ago. "Ernie" to his friends; "Honest Ernest" in his absence. The latter *nom de guerre* was sarcasm based on Ernie's penchant for sharp dealing and questionable acquisitions. In most other places in the world, Ernie's arrival would have generated suspicion generally, and at least a chat with the local authorities specifically. It wasn't just his appearance; he looked like a blond Grizzly Adams. It was the fact that he just wandered into the community about the time things started disappearing, and didn't seem to live anywhere in particular. But in a beach town, especially this beach town, Ernie wasn't regarded as overly peculiar, and was gradually accepted.

Ernie Brown, before his appearance at Pensacola

Beach, had been a student majoring in psychology at the University of North Texas. After four years, and the accumulation of ninety academic hours and one hundred and seventy "quality points," it came to him that he was not cut out to be another B.F. Skinner, or anybody else with an advanced degree in psychology for that matter. Aside from the obvious reasons – that he didn't quite have a 2.0 GPA and was on "double tough, bring up your grade point average in one semester or get out of school forever" scholastic probation – part of his revelation had been generated as a result of watching reruns of Kung Fu: he was meant to wander the earth doing good and having way neat adventures.

    Wandering south to Dallas, he learned many things. Among these insights were: money is almost essential, nobody wants to give a lift to a guy who looks like Grizzly Adams disguised as Kwai Chang Caine, Dallas police are not friendly and accepting, and walking barefoot beside a highway is not fun or enlightening. Meditating on these truths while being escorted through Dallas County by a particularly unfriendly and unaccepting police officer, Ernie extrapolated a yet higher truth: he must go where it was warm, easy to walk barefooted, and the police don't run you out of town – a beach.

    Swallowing his esthetic pride, he used part of what little money he had bilked from his parents and bought a pair of tennis shoes at a suburban K-Mart. This lone act, Ernie believed, changed his karma, for shortly thereafter he was picked up by a sailor, apparently drunk or stoned, who was headed for Pensacola Naval Air Station. En route, the sailor told stories of a beautiful island with sugar-white sand and easy living. This was clearly a sign as far as Ernie was concerned, and twelve hours later, Ernie's new friend dropped him at the Pensacola side of the Three Mile Bridge.

Three Mile Bridge is the first of two bridges, separated by the mainland peninsula town of Gulf Breeze, forming the western gateway to Santa Rosa Island. The island is a twenty-eight-mile-long sliver of pure white quartz sand bound easterly by the town of Navarre Beach, westerly by a pre-Civil War fort, Fort Pickens, to the north by Santa Rosa Sound, and to the south by the Gulf of Mexico. Most of it falls inside the Gulf Islands National Seashore, but the epicenter of the island is Pensacola Beach, a general designation that includes Casino Beach, Quietwater Beach, a double handful of houses, several hotels, and a mindboggling number of condominiums. This community of roughly five thousand permanent residents and an astronomical number of seasonal visitors would now incorporate the personage of Honest Ernest Brown.

Although occasionally people grimaced at his body odor, it was gratifying that no one seemed to regard him as strange. On the other hand, money was still a necessity, and Ernie might have starved had he not found a mentor.

It was his second night at the beach, and he had just enough money for maybe one more fish sandwich. As he unfurled his bedroll and crawled under the pier at Quietwater Beach, he stumbled over a body. Presuming the body was a dead body, he swallowed his revulsion and commenced to rifle through the corpse's pockets. "God forgive me, but he doesn't need it anymore," whispered Ernie.

"Well, He may forgive you, but I'm gonna cut your goddamn liver out, if you don't get your thievin' hands off me," roared the body.

For the first time since he was a very young child, Ernie wet himself.

"Jesus Christ, mister. You scared the shit outta me," Ernie exclaimed. "I thought you were dead."

"Well, I ain't dead, and you're not gettin' my stuff either," snapped the former body.

"Hey, man, I would'na stole your stuff if I'd known you were alive. I just thought that if you were dead, you wouldn't need it, and I sure did," apologized Ernie.

"Well, then, just leave me alone and go on about your business," the former body concluded and rolled over, to sleep apparently.

Ernie, having nothing better to do, moved away a bit from the former body and followed suit.

The sun came up early on the beach and, unfortunately, so did the tide. Ernie awoke with a start from a dream about wetting himself while being chased through the snow by a zombie. The zombie part wasn't clear, but the wetting was a rising tide, and he was indeed wet and cold.

"Hee, hee, hee, hee. Looks like you're all wet, Mr.

Robber," sniggered the former body.

Ernie's first reaction was anger. *Fuck you, old man*, he thought. But that probably wouldn't do anybody any good and, besides, he probably did look pretty funny. At that moment, it was either laugh or cry, so Ernie chose the former and began to laugh hysterically until he did, in fact, have tears rolling from his eyes. Strangely enough, the former body no longer seemed to see the humor.

"What's the problem?" Ernie queried. "Don't think it's funny? It's funny as hell. I'm a thousand miles from home, under a pier with a guy I thought was dead, soaking wet, and I don't have enough money to buy a fuckin' fish sandwich. Major yuk, don't you think?"

"No, kid, I guess I don't," said the former body. His eyes clearly underscored his feelings. Like maybe he'd seen it before; maybe he was seeing himself twenty years ago. "Look, kid, I can spot you a fish sandwich, and teach you how to get what you need. What do you say we buddy up? Folks call me Beachcomber Bart," he said, extending his hand.

What the hell, thought Ernie, *can't lose anything*.

As Ernie moved to take his hand, Bart pulled his hand up and away, closing his fist and pointing behind himself with his thumb. "Hee, hee, hee, hee! Fooled ya. Hee, hee. First lesson, don't trust nobody."

Oh, Christ, thought Ernie, looking skyward. But thereafter Bart proved to be as good as his word, springing for a fish sandwich at a beach bar near the old pier, or where the old pier used to be. Apparently it was blown away by a hurricane, but the longtime locals still used it as a reference point anyway.

As they ate, Bart began his graduate course in beach survival. "The first thing you need to know is a good fence. You see, if you're gonna live the beach life, you need to know where to sell things you... eh... find. I'll take you by and introduce you. She won't deal with just anybody.

"The next thing you need is a stash place. You may... eh... come on things 'most any time of day, but you don't take 'em to Annie – that's her name – any time except early in the mornin'. Ya see, most of the action on the beach takes place after noon and into the night. This is mostly a vacation place. People partyin' late and sleepin' late. Around now, six, seven in the mornin', nobody's out and about. Even the beach patrol doesn't get cranked 'til nine or ten. Point is, you need a place to stash your... eh... findings 'til you can take 'em down to Annie. Gotta be a place where some other... eh... entrepreneur," he winked, "won't find it. Don't want any kids stumblin' over it either.

"Now you can't just go out there and walk off with anything. City fathers won't stand for this place gettin' a reputation that scares tourists off. Start that kinda thievin' and things'll get mighty hot mighty quick. Bad for all of us, and especially bad for you. Slidell Goodbee, he's the sheriff, can be none-too-gentle with troublemakers. Some ol' boys have just disappeared. Some say he ran 'em out of town. Some say there's a lot of water out there." He nodded toward the gulf. "Myself, wouldn't bet either way. So you follow the Rule of the Pig. Know what that is?"

Ernie shook his head in the negative, savoring the last bite of fish sandwich.

"You can take a little, and get away with it. But if you get greedy, piggish, they'll get ya, and come down hard. That's it. The Rule of the Pig. Don't be a pig, and you'll make out OK.

"So what you do is look for stuff that could've been lost, and just kinda help it along. Beach stuff left out. Could've just been swept out to sea. Who knows? Folks don't go reportin' somethin' like that when it don't turn up. Annie'll pay you ten cents on the dollar for stuff like that. Put it away for two weeks, and resell it. People who lost it are already back in Cleveland. Don't even miss it.

"On the other hand, stuff missin' out of a car with a smashed window… Well, that's a different story. Those folks'll be in Slidell's office 'fore the glass stops tinklin'.

"Best time for beachcombin' is at night. If stuff's on the beach at night, it might really be lost. In a pinch, around six or so in the evenin' will work for little stuff. Folks inside takin' showers, gettin' ready to go out or fix dinner. But it's got to be little stuff that you can hide. Can't go luggin' a beach chair down the beach. Someone'll get suspicious."

Ernie nodded his head, but asked, "How come the sheriff puts up with you… us at all? Why not just run us all out? Clean up the beach entirely?"

"Well, first problem is, can't clean it up completely. Who wants to spend their vacation in church? Ya see what I'm sayin'? People want to come some place where they can blow off a little steam. Break the law a little. And they want a place with a little "local color." That's where we come in. Might as well go to DisneyWorld if you want squeaky clean.

"Second thing is, this place has a long history of... I guess what you'd call tolerance. This place is called the Emerald Coast. It's also called the Redneck Riviera, and it's also called the Gay Riviera. Gettin' the idea? We got the Navy, the rednecks, the Bible thumps, blacks, gays, and regular folks. All here at the same time. All sharin' the beach, and gettin' along. Not sayin' there's no friction, but for the most part, it's live and let live. Everybody seems pretty content to leave everybody else alone, if nobody bothers anybody. Beachcombers," he winked again, "don't quite fit there, but we're close enough, and you start makin' value judgments, the next thing you know, Ralph Reed is runnin' the show.

"So there you are. You stick with me for a while, learnin', then we'll turn you loose on your own."

And that's the way things went for a couple of seasons: Bart the Beachcomber and Honest Ernest. But one day, for God-only-knows-what reason, Ernie decided he wanted to leave "the life." He got a real job, helping with a beach concession operation. Kind of like a lower echelon Slidell Goodbee, Ernie was good at it. He saved some money and, after a while, went in business for himself. Became a member of the legitimate beach community. He eventually had several beach equipment concessions, and things were going smoothly until the night of the "Southern Lights."

Chapter III

    The night of the Southern Lights, Ernie had gone to Flounder's Chowder & Ale House, an island restaurant and bar, to witness their bikini contest and reggae band.
    This was a weekly extravaganza specifically designed to recruit sun worshipers from the beach before they could pack up their stuff and head for wherever they came from. The recruitment was accomplished by means of a small aircraft which circled the beach continuously, pulling a large banner announcing the event to anyone who wasn't deaf and blind. Ernie had often thought that, after two or three passes, it might have been more effective to let everyone know that if they'd go to Flounder's, the guy would stop flying over the beach and bothering people. But nobody had asked him.
    The bikini contest had been nothing special. The "reg-

gae band" had been good, but apparently knew only one reggae tune, the one used by the Jamaica Tourist Bureau to lure people to their island: "Come to Jamaica ...."

The whole thing would have been just another night in paradise not getting laid, if it hadn't been for a tourist lady who had had one too many "diesel fuels," the house special knockout drink.

Mistaking Ernie for Grizzly Adams perhaps, the tourist lady dragged Ernie onto the sand dance floor, where they stayed, between diesel fuels, until the band quit.

The tourist lady, whose name turned out to be Helen something, was about forty, but very well preserved, and even kind of attractive – more handsome than pretty. Helen explained that she was in Pensacola for a nursing convention that ended today, and she was looking to blow off some steam before heading back to Beaumont.

Ernie wasn't sure whether she meant "blow off steam" as in get drunk and dance, or "blow off steam" as in get drunk and screw. But as the night progressed and her syncopated gyrations to the music became a contact sport, he concluded the latter. As the band began to pack instruments, Ernie and Helen grabbed two diesel fuels and headed for Ernie's house, with Helen giving Ernie a pelvic massage on the way.

Helen proved to be both athletic and attentive. To Ernie's exhausted relief, as the morning began to gray the night sky, their love-making ended. It seemed like only an hour or two had passed when the "boom, boom, boom" of a U-boat shelling Pensacola Beach brought Ernie to consciousness.

Why would a German gunboat be shelling the beach instead of the Navy base? These were Ernie's first thoughts, as he realized that someone was actually pounding on his door and that the pounding had been confabulated into gunboat shelling by his unconscious mind. Noting the drool on the pillow beside Helen's open mouth, Ernie concluded that Helen was a sound sleeper; he slipped on his boat shorts from the night before and made his way to the door.

Ernie's house was at the east end of the island, two blocks north of Via de Luna Drive, a one-story cinderblock product of the '50s that had managed to survive Hurricane Opal, apparently by burrowing itself deep in the sand. At least that was how it appeared when the police allowed residents back on the island subsequent to the big blow. The owner at that time, presumably thinking that selling low rather than digging deep was the best deal, let Ernie have the property for next to nothing, and Ernie, for the first time in his life, became a member of the landed gentry, kinda.

It had taken three months to dig out, clean out, and wash up what was left of the house, but after all the cleaning, the house proved quite adequate for a *nouveau* capitalist. Plus, the property had access to the sound side of the island, and one day Ernie planned to build a slip for the boat he hoped to buy. A used twenty-eight or thirty-foot sloop would do nicely. Then, of course, he'd have to learn to sail. But that was fine with Ernie. His dream of Kwai Chang had somehow melded into a dream of Ernest Hemingway starring himself.

"Boom, boom, boom," came the knock again. Not only was this guy irritating, he was also persistent.

Who in his right mind would come banging on a dude's door at the crack of dawn? It better not be some lost tourist looking for directions, Ernie thought.

Through the film of last night's diesel fuel, the significance of his own question caused the fur on the back of Ernie's neck to rise. Before answering the door, he slipped a reefing knife into his pocket and peered cautiously out the front window. He couldn't see who was actually doing the knocking, but what he did see caused an involuntary shudder. Slidell Goodbee's black-and-white unit was parked right in the middle of what passed for Ernie's driveway.

This could not be good news, he thought as he cautiously opened the door. "Morning, Sheriff. Kinda early to be knocking on a door, isn't it?" *Unless, of course, he's serving some kind of warrant.* Ernie cringed at the possibility.

Something about too little sleep and being confronted by a mostly naked, blond, Grizzly-Adams-looking guy, who reeked of stale booze and sex, made Slidell's job less pleasant than it could have been. Lord knows he didn't want to go inside. It could only smell worse, and who knew what or who he might find? "Honest Ernest. Would you mind stepping out here? I need to talk to you."

Ernie didn't mind this at all. The last thing he wanted

was Slidell Goodbee loose in his house. His head was too foggy to remember if there was any evil weed laying around, and he didn't care to have Slidell surveying the ruins of last night's frolic. Certainly Helen Whatever didn't bargain for anything Slidell Goodbee might be about to do.

As they moved in the general direction of the squad car, Ernie tried his best to shake the cobwebs out of his head and to avoid the grass burrs which were everywhere, even if a person did take care of his lawn.

"Honest Ernest, I've got some bad news for you." Slidell paused to let that sink in.

Ernie wondered just what kind of jail time he might be looking at.

"Someone blew up one of your beach boxes last night."

This bad news, relative to the bad news Ernie had been fearing, caused him to release the breath he had been holding, and expel air mightily. "Whew!!!" went Ernie.

Very curious reaction from a man receiving bad news, Slidell considered. *Yuk!!! What a case of butt breath*, was his next thought. "Hoped you might know something about it. You see, two people were killed."

This news caused Ernie to suck the breath back in and, to Slidell's disgust, release it again. "Are you kiddin', man?" exclaimed Ernie, genuinely shocked.

Slidell gave Ernie one of those half-frowns and turned his head slightly, as if to say *Yeah, asshole. I came out here at the crack of dawn to do a little jukin' and jivin' 'cause we're such good friends.*

"Hmmm. I guess you're not kiddin'," said Ernie, mostly to himself. Then, "I don't know nothin' about it, Sheriff. I, like, just woke up. Who got killed? Which box was it?"

Even if Dallas had told Slidell something, which it hadn't because he hadn't called them yet, Slidell wouldn't have told Honest Ernest Brown unless he was in the process of confronting him with murder and arson. It wasn't that he didn't like Ernie. He just remembered what Ernie used to be, and probably still was. "Don't know about the victims yet, but the box is the one across from Peg Leg's."

Ernie "hmmmed" and put his hand on his chin and looked up at the sky for a couple of minutes before saying, "Sorry, can't help you, Sheriff. Would if I could, but I don't have any idea who would torch my box. Maybe something will come to me later."

With that, Slidell gave Ernie the "suspicious cop" look, one of his cards, and said "Call me, etcetera," as he got in his car, thankfully leaving this bohemian behind.

Ernie had pretty much forgotten Helen as he watched the sheriff drive away and, turning to go in, he began to consider seriously the "who" and "why" of his destroyed box.

The beach paraphernalia rental business wasn't exactly like real estate sales, but there was a fair element of competition involved. Probably most people never thought about it, looking at a handful of chairs and umbrellas and a tanned dude lying on the beach attending them, but at sixteen dollars per day rental for each rig, seven days a week, for three to five months, the money could be significant, especially as the number of rigs increased. Based on ten rigs, a season could add up – fourteen thousand to twenty-four thousand dollars for the year, and for every ten more rigs you had, you could double it.

Given the income potential, a person might wonder why this kind of opportunity wasn't more widely known. The answer was twofold: beach people and work. Most people who come to the beach are thinking about anything but work. Of that small group who actually know about the business, a much smaller portion of them want to really work. Of those who want to work, only a small number of them are capable of the kind of work involved. That is to say, the obvious is only the tip of the iceberg, but even that still requires a genial and patient person. You've got to make the sale to the beachers, and you've got to be patient when they insist on extra attention or persist in occupying the equipment up to and beyond the time deadline. Plus, if you have more than one contract, you have management responsibilities which, considering who your employees are, increases problems geometrically.

But first you have to get the "contract," the entitlement to operate in a specific place, and then it gets crazy. First, the beach is public property, which would seem to dictate a partnership with the government, and it does, to some extent. Five percent of profits to the Santa Rosa Island Authority and, of course, state and local tax: seven percent. But that only gives the operator a kind of general authority to be on the beach. To actually be somewhere in particular, you have to get written permission for exclusive operation in front of any given hotel or condominium. These entities apparently have some sort of penumbra of ownership that extends from their actual property to the water's edge. Getting this authority requires the ability to deal with a range of people, from high-powered corporate executives with final authority for a decision to give such a contract, to semi-illiterate beach curmudgeons who can't say "boo" without two-thirds approval of a homeowners' association.

Finally, the reverse twist, which makes the whole thing very very curious indeed, is that if for some reason you are unable to perform your part of the bargain (have the chairs ready to go on demand), the next operator down the beach will likely be given the opportunity to step into your shoes immediately. This last little wrinkle opens the door to skullduggery. In the beach rental business, there are certain times of vast profit: Memorial Day, July 4th, Labor Day. If the operator next door had, let's say, an unfortunate accident, like all his rigs were blown into South Alabama, then you could take over the unfortunate's spot until he could perform. If the accident happened to occur just prior to one of the dollar bonanza dates, a person might double his profit for the year.

These were the thoughts that were ricocheting through the diesel sludge of Ernie's head as he schlocked out of the bright sunshine and into his house.

"Honey? Where's my little beach banana?" came the

throaty moan from the direction of his bedroom.

Oh, Lord, thought Ernie, *why can't they just disappear in the morning?* But he saw his duty, and he didn't shrink from it, so to speak.

An hour later, Ernie stood in the shower letting the warm water wash the night away. He had promised to write and visit if he ever got up to... somewhere, and he waved goodbye as Helen drove toward Navarre. By the time he realized she was going in the wrong direction, it was too late.

Hell, she'll figure it out, he had concluded, heading back into his house. Now the only thing on his mind, other than major skull cramps, was Percy Meriweather VanAlstine, known with varying degrees of antipathy as "Scudder."

Chapter IV

The first time Donny Ray VanAlstine ever laid eyes on his son, it was visiting day for Jester Unit at the Texas Department of Corrections. Janie Meriweather, Donny Ray's common law wife, had brought their newborn up for his first "get acquainted" visit with Dad. As it turned out, this was a particularly appropriate setting for father and son, as they would throughout the years have frequent visits in such an environment, occasionally changing sides of the plexiglass window.

"Ain't he just the cutest thing, Donny Ray? Momma says he's got your eyes and my nose. Uncle Bart says he looks just like Grandpa. But I think he looks just like you," gushed Janie.

Donny Ray just looked puzzled and grinned, using all

three of his teeth. "Whadja name him?"

"Well, Donny Ray, Junior, of course," replied Janie, hoping the name would make Donny Ray more inclined to claim the baby. There was some question in this area, as Janie Meriweather wasn't exactly anyone's idea of marital fidelity. However, she had reasoned, a girl's got needs, and if her old man can't stay out of prison, well...

Donny Ray continued to stare at the baby, apparently puzzling something out in his head, and finally said, "Yeah, well, I guess he's mine. But name him Percy."

"Percy!? What kinda damn name is that? Sounds like a fag poet to me," exclaimed Janie.

"Well, that's how it's gonna be. If his last name's gonna be VanAlstine, then his first name's gonna be Percy, and you can stick any other names in there that you want."

Janie didn't think much of that, but it was better than having a child without his father's, or some father's, name. "OK, but his middle name's gonna be Meriweather, after my side of the family," Janie countered.

After a bit of silence, Donny seemed satisfied. "Done then. The boy's a VanAlstine: Percy Meriweather VanAlstine. Kinda has a ring to it, and he is a cute little scudder," pronounced Donny Ray.

The pronouncement proved prophetic. The baby definitely turned out to be a VanAlstine, and the nickname "Scudder" stuck. Donny Ray genuinely liked the nickname, and Janie couldn't bring herself to call him Percy.

It had been Donny Ray's plan from the beginning that

Scudder become self-sufficient as soon as possible because, in his heart, Donny Ray knew his son wouldn't have the debatable benefit of his guidance. Donny Ray didn't plan on changing his ways, and that meant he'd frequently be the guest of the ol' Crossbar Hotel. Drawing on his rather limited resources, Donny Ray recalled a song by Johnny Cash called "A Boy Named Sue," where the boy's father had named him Sue so he would "have to get tough or die." Donny Ray figured "Percy" would have the same effect, and it did.

From his first interaction with other boys, Scudder had to prove he was tough, and fortunately he was. Unfortunately, he wasn't very big. The net result was that by the time Scudder got to high school, nobody called him Percy because they'd have to fight him every day until they stopped. To the bigger, tougher guys, this got old: "Sorry, Melissa, I can't walk you home. I've gotta go beat the shit outta Scudder again." Finally, everybody just called him Scudder. It was easier that way. Besides, "Scudder" kind of fit him; there was something weaselish about the name.

After a year of high school, Scudder quit. All new teachers called him Percy, at least on the first day of class, and he couldn't fight them. Plus, he didn't see much use in school. He was a VanAlstine, and all VanAlstines were hustlers. Although Donny Ray was in and out of prison much of the time, some uncle or another was around to explain to Scudder how the world worked and how a man got things done. What his uncles told him didn't have anything to do with algebra, and Scudder couldn't see how knowing how to recite the

Gettysburg Address was going to put money in his pocket.

After he left school, detention hall became juvenile hall, as Scudder fast became a petty criminal. Stealing was what he did, and with the family tutelage, he became pretty good. Nevertheless, the fine art of thieving is a learning process by trial and error, which meant he was frequently "detained" by law enforcement. Shortly after his eighteenth birthday, he erred by getting caught with stolen goods that exceeded the misdemeanor level, and with his lengthy juvenile record, he was admitted to the graduate school of criminology: Ferguson Unit, Texas Department of Criminal Justice - Institutional Division, or simply "TDC" to those in that arena of life.

In Ferguson, he met Rufus, a large black man, who had both a wealth of knowledge about thieving and a predilection for young white boys. At first the idea of becoming Rufus's "bitch" was not his ego ideal, but the idea kinda grew on him, not to mention that the alternative was not being at all. Besides that, nobody jacked with Rufus's bitch, and with the development of this new relationship, prison life became more bearable. With all his thieving and fighting, Scudder had never had a girlfriend – not counting "Palmella" – and after he got used to the idea, Rufus wasn't so bad. He even grew quite fond of Rufus, in a guy sort of way.

Rufus had not only had a deprived, rudderless upbringing, but he had also been a gang member. Among the many privileges of gang membership was straight no-shit instruction on how to get business done. Rufus knew how to steal, and he had only got caught, according to Rufus, because some punk had ratted him out. This would be taken care of later, and Rufus had learned from it: operate solo and don't let nobody know your business.

A person couldn't say it was an idyllic two years, but time did pass. Because Rufus's particular criminal episode also involved murder, he would be a guest of the state for a while longer than Scudder. So Scudder bid him farewell, promised to write, and hit the street armed with a fine working knowledge of the stealing business.

Scudder also was wondering if he was destined to be a fag now. If so, he thought, maybe he'd start going by Percy. He'd have to wait and see.

Because he had elected to work in one of the prison industries, he had accumulated some money, but he wasn't sure exactly what he was going to do with it. He didn't drink, gamble, or chase women. So all he really needed was food and a place to sleep. One thing he was sure of, he didn't want to stay in Texas. Rufus had said Florida was crawling with crooks, and it seemed only reasonable to go live with your own kind. Buying a bus ticket for the closest place in Florida, he appropriated something to wear that didn't look like TDC issue, and headed out for Pensacola, a name he found amusing.

One of the first things Scudder noticed about life on the outside was that the transportation was much better than the prison bus, and he went quickly to sleep on something softer than anything he had been on for two years. When he awoke, the bus was pulling into a large lighted terminal, with the driver explaining that this was the end of the road.

New to the area, in fact new to any area except his hometown, Scudder had no idea where he was, but figured from the buildings he was near city center. Turning south by chance, he came upon a convenience store in a few blocks. "Groovin' Noovin'" was its name, which also amused him. How bad could a place be with all these funny names? he asked himself. He bought a Coke and lifted a candy bar, then went outside to sit on the curb and think.

What Scudder didn't know was that he had arrived in Pensacola on Friday night of Memorial Day Weekend. Another thing Scudder didn't know was that Pensacola Beach had been dubbed the Gay Riviera mostly because of the number of gays and lesbians who flock to this area of Northwest Florida on Memorial Day Weekend. Had he known these things, it would not have made any difference, but it would have given what happened next a more meaningful context.

As Scudder polished off the last bite of his Baby Ruth, a big white Cadillac convertible pulled up next to him at the curb. He didn't think much about this because it was, after all, a parking lot.

However, a large, very tanned guy with blond ringlets of hair gave him a coy look and said, "Hi there."

"Hi there," Scudder reciprocated, but with a markedly different intonation.

"What's a handsome young fellow like yourself doing sitting alone on a curb?" said Blondie.

Scudder had never thought of himself as handsome, or ugly, or anything really, but the attention pleased him. "Just sittin'. Just got into town, and I was wonderin' where to go."

"Well now, guy, why don't you come with me to a party with some friends of mine? My place is out on the beach, and it's going to be great fun," suggested Blondie.

What the hell, Scudder thought, *why not?* "Sure. Scudder's the name. What do I call you?"

"My name is William, but my good friends call me Billy Boy," explained Billy Boy.

Driving over the Bob Sikes Bridge to Pensacola Beach, the warm salty gulf air flowed around Scudder, causing his mood to soar for the first time in a long while, maybe ever.

This is truly heaven, he thought. *This is where I want to stay.*

The CD player in the car played some strange music that sure wasn't blues, but he liked it just the same. He was wondering when the last time was that he'd heard anything but rap and blues, as Billy Boy took a right on Fort Pickens Road. Two minutes later, the car stopped at the Surf's Up Tower, and Billy Boy escorted Scudder to a large suite on the top floor overlooking the Gulf of Mexico.

When Billy Boy opened the door, Scudder was almost knocked backwards by the music and the gush of marijuana smoke.

"Hi, party folk," Billy Boy shouted over the bedlam.

"This is Scudder. He's my new friend."

The first thing Scudder noticed as Billy Boy escorted him to the bar was that this certainly was a party. People dancing and frolicking everywhere. The second thing he noticed was that all these people were male, except for one or two who could have been either.

Scudder had never met a real homosexual, but he figured this was them. "Fuckin' queers" his uncles had called them, always with a look of disdain. But if there was something wrong with them, Scudder couldn't see it. They all seemed to be having fun, and they weren't threatening. Scudder knew threatening.

He didn't really jump naked into the party; he decided to just go along and see. As it turned out, nothing much happened. Everybody seemed to get drunk or stoned, and towards sunrise he ended up in bed with Billy Boy. Seemed normal enough to Scudder.

Sometime the next afternoon, he awoke in the most wonderful bed he had ever been in, with Billy Boy beckoning him to one of the most wonderful breakfasts he had ever had.

What, he wondered, *did my uncles see wrong here? Well, fuck my uncles. I'll take Billy Boy over them any day.*

The weekend ended, but the relationship didn't. Turned out that Billy Boy was William Turman, a big deal lawyer in town. He kept this place for weekends, and told Scudder he could stay until he could get on his feet. As the relationship progressed, both came to know much about the other. Scudder gradually came to realize that this was a familiar arrangement, but by another name. Scudder was to be Billy Boy's bitch. But that was OK. Scudder knew that good things could flow from such a setup, and from the perspective of a kid with no future, good things did result.

As it happened, the Surf's Up had lost its last beach concessionaire. Billy Boy arranged for Scudder to get the spot, bought the rentals, and took time to explain the process of doing business, real-world-style. The arrangement could have been good for Scudder and Billy Boy, but Scudder was ambitious and he wasn't quite sure he wanted to be a homosexual. Something about mostly naked women with gulf tans made Scudder doubt his commitment. Also, his breeding, or lack thereof, ran too deep. You couldn't just stop being a criminal after twenty years, and turn into a law-abiding homosexual. Things began to turn up missing, and Billy Boy was no Beachcomber Bart. Guests lost jewelry, other beach concessionaires had things missing that looked a lot like the stuff Scudder was using, several cars were broken into. Annie refused to deal with Scudder. Slidell Goodbee's attention was inevitably drawn in the direction of the Surf's Up.

For these reasons, when Ernie arrived to survey the damage to his beach box, he wasn't surprised to see Slidell's cruiser parked at the Surf's Up Tower.

Chapter V

From the air, the beach must have looked like some kind of artist's rendering in black and white. Maybe like "Ink Drop on White Paper." Not that the local servicemen were thinking about artists' renderings when they did the daily "bikini patrol." The bikini patrol was so named because it consisted of helicopter gunships, of the various branches of the service located in the Pensacola area, flying forebodingly down the length of the beach, peculiarly at times coincident with prime sunbathing time. The flyovers were actually supposed to be a Coast Guard function to protect our shores from invasion, or drug smuggling, although neither seemed likely to occur on Pensacola Beach. Of course, who's to say that a drug boat wouldn't pull up to a beach crowded with sun lovers, and unload jillions of dollars worth of cocaine?

In any case, it didn't look like an artist's rendering to Ernie. What had once been a tacky rectangular blue box was now a large black smudge on the uniquely pristine sand of the Emerald Coast. As he circled the black area, looking for anything that might have survived the explosion, Ernie stopped on a smaller smudge, then jumped, stumbling to the side when he realized that the little smudge must have been from the two people who were killed.

Nothing left here, he thought, as he wondered what his insurance policy said about explosion coverage. Down the beach a couple hundred yards, he could see a man in uniform beside a skinny scruffy-looking guy. He assumed it was Slidell Goodbee talking to Scudder VanAlstine about what he knew of the explosion.

This, in fact, was true.

"So, Scudder, what were you up to last night," queried the sheriff, "around, say, eight o'clock?"

"Well, let's see." Scudder pretended to think hard. He knew this would be coming, and had his alibi all in place, but he didn't want it to appear that way to Goodbee. "I'd got all my stuff put away, and went in about six-thirty or seven. Yeah, about eight I'd've been having a beer with Mr. Turman."

Slidell knew the rumor that Scudder was a "kept man," but he could never quite square it with the way Scudder came across. Scudder was more shiv than gay blade. There wasn't much Slidell didn't know about most of the locals on the island, especially if he had questions about them. After noticing Scudder hanging around for a few months, and after he set up shop as a beach merchant, Slidell had checked with the Santa Rosa Island Authority. To be a beach merchant, you had to get the OK from the Authority, and that meant giving them your social security number, true name, and brief history. Although Scudder had left out the part about prison, given Scudder's real name, it was easy enough for Slidell to run him through N.C.I.C., the National Crime Information Computer. Bingo! Scudder was an ex-con on parole out of Texas.

"And I suppose Mr. Turman will verify that?" pushed Slidell.

"Well, sure. I guess. No reason for him not to, me being there and all," responded Scudder defensively. "How come you're talking to me, anyway?"

"Well, now, Percy, that's my job, isn't it? You know how the drill works, don't you, Percy?" baited Slidell.

Scudder just looked, suppressing the anger.

"You know how the police do," said Slidell, hitting the "po" in "police" hard. "Even in Texas, huh?"

"Listen, Sheriff, I did my time. Paid my debt to society. I'm an upstanding citizen now. You got no reason to be rousting me."

"Uh huh. Been a lot of stuff going on here since you hit town, Percy. Stuff that didn't happen before you got here. Just makes me curious," challenged Slidell, giving Scudder the suspicious cop look.

"Just 'cause shit happens don't mean I'm good for it.

"There's lots of lowlifes on this beach," Scudder answered, looking off in the direction of Ernie.

Slidell really couldn't argue with that, but continued giving Scudder the look anyway. "Just bear in mind that I'll always be about a half-step behind you, and if you stumble, I'll be on you like stink on shit." With that, he paused and, as he turned to go, suggested, "You keep in touch now, Percy."

Just because it always seemed to work with Columbo, after taking a few steps, Slidell turned, which caused Scudder some embarrassment, as he was in the process of sticking his tongue out at the departing sheriff. "Oh, yeah," remarked Slidell, trying to ignore Scudder's withdrawing tongue, "how'd you learn about explosives?"

For a moment, Slidell thought it was going to work. It seemed like Scudder was about to explain, but caught himself. "I don't know nothing about explosives. Now leave me alone, Sheriff, less you got somethin' on me."

With that exchange, Slidell actually did leave. As Scudder watched him go, he was thinking that he'd made the bomb just like Rufus taught him. Dug a hole under the beach box, used the delay fuse, and ten minutes later: "KABOOM!" Too bad about those people, though. But hey, like he told the sheriff, shit happens.

*****

Five miles north, William Turman was glancing through the *Pensacola News Journal* as he drank Sunday morning tea with his buttered muffin. Frowning as the ringing phone interrupted his Sunday morning ritual, he answered "Hell-O!" emphasizing the "o."

"Turman? Tanner here," announced Farley Tanner, abruptly. "You hear the news?"

"News? What news?" replied Turman. "Why are you calling me here? We're not even supposed to know each other. What if someone else had answered? What if, you know, the line is bugged?"

"Don't be an idiot, Turman. Who would bug your phone? You're a respectable real estate lawyer. Who cares what real estate lawyers do? And if it hadn't been you, I'd have hung up. The news is, someone blew up a beach box across from Peg Leg's and killed two people. And the bad news is, it was probably your boy," exclaimed Farley, and paused.

"Why would you think it was Scudder?" defended Turman.

"Who else? Ever since he showed up, there's been a minor crime wave on the island, and, in this case, he's the only one with a motive," explained Farley. "Word is that Slidell Goodbee was out on the island talking to him this morning, and that's bad. We don't need the sheriff pokin' around out there. No telling what he might stumble onto."

This time when Farley paused, there was only empty silence.

Farley continued, his voice deliberately menacing, "If you don't reign that hoss in, I'll have to take care of your boy toy."

Another pause.

"You copy on that, Billy Boy?"

"I'll have a conversation with him. It won't happen again," he promised glumly.

"We'll see, Turman. But it better not," deadpanned Farley, as he hung up the phone.

*****

Farley Tanner hadn't always been a lay minister/carpenter. Before that, he had sold boats in Saint Petersburg. Before that, he dabbled in the drug trade between the Caribbean and Miami. Farley, who came into this world as Thomas Edward Whiting, had first been introduced to the devil on a church tour of the Leeward Islands along the Caribbean Sea. The idea had been that young people from the Full Gospel Church of Jesus would charter a boat and go from island to island spreading The Word.

This had been great fun, and partially successful, until the group reached the Dominican Republic. Farley, or Thomas, as he was known at the time, was the main draw for the group, due to his skills as an orator. He couldn't sing all that well, but with backup by the "Soul Reapers," as the choir was known, he could stumble through. The drill was that the Soul Reapers would sing for thirty minutes, Farley would preach for an hour, the Soul Reapers would wrap it up, and they'd eat dinner as guests of the locals while seeking converts.

The poverty of the Dominican Republic was only surpassed by that of Haiti on the other side of the island, which caused great empathy on Farley's part for the islanders. Due to the fact that Farley was the star, and also that he was the only member of the group who spoke Spanish, he was placed in close proximity to their hostess. Her natural good looks, and Farley's emotional predisposition toward all the islanders, caused an immediate attraction that Farley had never before experienced.

Apparently, believing Farley was a man of importance, the attraction was mutual. No one thought anything about the hostess whispering in Farley's ear throughout the meal, and, for the most part, it had been legitimate. It was only as the evening passed that the hostess's whispers became more amorous than religious.

After dinner, some clumsy attempts at polite conversation, and a few verses of "Bringing in the Sheaves," Farley made some excuse about having to stay behind to discuss the fine points of the group's beliefs. Farley assured the chaperone that all would be fine, and he'd be back on the boat as soon as Guadalupe, the hostess, understood, and hopefully accepted, The Word.

The steel drums, the full moon, and Lupe's hot blood did result in a conversion. Farley's. His life in Littleton, Georgia, had been fine, but nothing like this. Farley became a man that night under the full moon, as the tropical breezes gently rocked the palm trees, and Lupe, not so gently, rocked Farley. As the first rays of light turned the horizon to flame, Farley made his decision. He would stay with Lupe forever, living the life of a simple islander. He slipped aboard ship and left a message for the chaperone: "I've found my mission here. Don't try to find me; I'll be fine. *Via con Dios* – Tommy."

Of course, the chaperone did try to find Tommy, but fifteen white kids and a chaperone just don't cut it in the "search for someone in a non-English-speaking country" game. Finally, with the chaperone wondering just what in the world he was going to tell Tommy's parents, they left. Tommy, now "Tomas," began to experience life as a "simple islander." It was horrible.

For starters, love among the masses was not so neat. With eight siblings, two parents, and a grandmother in the two-room house, passion diminished. Occasionally, they would get up and leave the house for the beach, but that was hot, sandy, and there were lots of mosquitoes who seemed to want to get involved in their love-making.

At first, Tomas was included in Lupe's family, as far as food and shelter went, but after days stretched to weeks, Lupe's father began to realize that Tomas was not a benefit, but a burden; no money coming in, and more food going out. And Grandmother began to make disparaging remarks just within Tomas's hearing about living as man and wife without the blessing of the church.

Responding to this not-so-subtle pressure, Tomas turned his hand to the only thing he knew: spreading The Word. He set up shop on the beach on Sunday mornings, preaching to the people as they went about their business. Because he was, in fact, quite a public speaker, he gradually attracted a following. The Beach Church, as Tomas's little, but growing, congregation came to be called, soon attracted the attention of the local officials. The problem was that Tomas's flock had grown to such proportions that they literally blocked the beach. This caused tourists to complain that they couldn't use the beach on Sunday mornings. Anything that bothered the tourists bothered the government. Tourism was a major source of income. Thus spurred into action, the local magistrate paid Tomas a visit to explain that if Tomas did not shut down, he would take a closer look at Tomas's visa.

Tomas didn't really take the news hard. The fact of the matter was that Tomas was thankful to be given the excuse to close down. Although the Beach Church had been wildly successful in terms of the numbers it attracted, the financial end had been something less than gratifying. What Tomas had overlooked was that the simple islanders were indeed dirt poor. When Tomas passed the collection plate, he would get nothing, and it wasn't because the congregation didn't want to give. The only result of Tomas's threats of fire and brimstone for those who didn't tithe was to make his followers look more forlorn. They just didn't have anything to give, even if it meant the loss of their immortal soul.

So Tomas wasn't too unhappy to give up his ministry, and began looking around for some other source of income, as Lupe's family began looking closer at him again. In spite of his determination, there was nothing. He couldn't fish; he didn't know how. He had never been any good with his hands, and he had long ago ruled out manual labor and begging on the street.

Besides, all those positions were taken by the natives.

In a flash of brilliance, he decided that perhaps being bilingual, plus being an American, he could work as a guide or a concierge for the big resorts. This seemed like the perfect thing to Tomas, but as soon as he contacted some of the big hotels, he was once again visited by the magistrate. This was a closed shop.

As one opportunity after another came to nothing, like so many rabbit trails, things on the homefront turned worse. Not only did pressure increase from the family, but he could also see that he had diminished in Lupe's eyes. Clearly, he was not the savior she had thought him to be.

By the opposite side of the same token, she was beginning to look more like an ignorant peasant than an island love goddess. It was pretty obvious that he should have stayed with his own kind, but in addition to lust, there was also pride. He couldn't bring himself to call Mommy and Daddy for money to come home, assuming they would be willing to help him out. He was pretty sure the news of his "fall" would now be common knowledge in Littleton. His mom might help, but his father was never a forgiving, or forgetting, man. There was face-saving involved here.

Nope. He was on his own at the end of his rope. The long walk on the short pier was looking like his only option, as he considered his situation and stared out at the Caribbean Sea. It was then that he was approached by Hernando Donellen, the local drug dealer, who had been waiting patiently for just this state of affairs to develop.

"Why so sad, Tomasito?" inquired Donellen gently from behind. He had judged this to be the time.

Tomas turned with a jump, and recognized Donellen immediately. "What's it to you, *Señor*? he answered. He had properly modulated his voice and used the title of respect, not because he really did respect this criminal, but he was afraid not to. Donellen had a reputation.

"What is it to me? Do you not think I am capable of sympathy for another human being?" Donellen answered. "I have observed you since your arrival on our island, and noted your fortunes have fared badly. Perhaps I could help?"

What it was to him, Tomas would shortly determine, was that Tomas had a U.S. passport in fine working order. He could enter and leave the States almost without question, and he was young and clean cut. Thomas Edward Whiting did not even come close to the DEA's "Drug Courier Profile." Donellen needed a mule, and Tomas looked like he was ripe for recruitment.

"Here," Donellen handed Tomas a one-hundred-peso note. "Take this. Just as a friend for now. There's lots more where that came from. You know my business. You know what I need. Think about it. Take your time."

Donellen was very clever. He was also very right. Tomas eyed him for a moment, and made a decision. It was just a gift involving no commitment for now, and he did need the money. He took the money. "Thank you, *Señor* Donellen," he said, as he headed off in the direction of Lupe's house.

"You know where to find me, Tomasito," said

Donellen as he thought, *Tomas will bite; he has no other choice.*

In six months, Tomas was making weekly trips to Miami, Houston, Phoenix, and New York. He was now a Bible salesman buying additional merchandise in the States. Although he was rarely detained at customs, when he was, he could talk God with the best of them. The few encounters Tomas experienced ended with profuse apologies by the government for suspecting a man of God.

At home, he had the grudging respect of the family, except Grandma, who insisted on addressing him as *cabeza diablo* (roughly, the devil's head). The rest of the family had to show respect. He was now their chief source of sustenance. But the smiling faces covered hearts of ice. They knew. He was no longer a man of God, or even a man of bungling integrity. Grandma was right.

Be that as it may, Tomas wasn't dull, either emotionally or intellectually. He knew what the family was feeling and, by and large, he felt the same toward them: nothing. He also knew that being a mule for a drug pusher was neither his goal in life nor something that would allow him to live as a free man for very long. He saved his money, and after one trip to Miami, he made the delivery and disappeared. Donellen was no doubt unhappy to lose a good mule, but basically they were even; no hard feelings.

Thomas Edward Whiting, aka Tomas, became Ward

Whiting, and after drifting for a while, settled down in Saint Petersburg.

While in the islands, he had learned a good bit about sailboats. He had had the use of Donellen's forty-five-foot Beneteau when he wasn't working, and had quickly developed a fondness for sailing. Big Ed Morresy, "the biggest yacht dealer on Florida's west coast," hadn't been too picky about references when "Ward" applied, and after deciding that Ward could talk the talk, Ed put him to work as a yacht salesman.

This job was a glove-like fit for Ward. He could indeed talk the talk, and in fairly short order, he became Big Ed's leading salesman. With success came money, and Ward was free with it.

Although Saint Petersburg has the reputation as the "old people capital" of the United States, there are many other factions in the area. One is the fast money boys, who operate just on the free-to-walk-around side of the law and prey on the seniors and any other likely subjects they can find. Ward found a place in this social order.

Things couldn't have been better for Ward. Big Ed was even talking partners in one of his deals. Then the U.S. declared its war on drugs. The DEA began rethinking some of the drug traffic routes, especially between the States and the Dominican Republic. It wasn't a big step to locate the former Thomas Edward Whiting, now operating under the name Ward Whiting, and when they left a card at Big Ed's, after narrowly missing him, Ward decided it was time for a change of life.

Drawing on his acquaintances in the underbelly of Saint Pete, he invested in a total identity package. He became Farley Gene Tanner, and high-tailed it north.

Chapter VI

As the sun's rays began to move to an angle that finally didn't seem directly vertical, Scudder watched the scarlet-toned tourists begin to examine their sun-ravaged bodies, as if something new had just occurred. Baring that particular shade of red, Scudder knew they had to be in pain, but they seemed delighted with their new skin color. Like anything but white was just fine. Never mind that they wouldn't be able to sleep tonight without air conditioning and hourly applications of Solarcaine.

Tourists, Scudder thought, *who knows what goes on in their heads?*

Despite his disgust for the kind of person who would try to squeeze a summer's worth of tanning into a weekend, Scudder's half-smile reflected a huge grin within. Business had been great today. He'd filled all his chairs, and had to rent some more from a guy down beach. He hated to pay the rental, but he could then jack up his charge, and still make some money. Too bad there wasn't any competition from next door, he smirked to himself.

It always seemed that on sunny days, the heat would keep baking forever. Then, as now, there was a detectable shift in the sun's angle, and the whole beach would begin a rapid cool toward evening. He watched the lobster-like couples begin gathering their gear for the trek back to the condominiums, and knew, as sure as most were leaving, one or two diehards would hang in until rental time was up. But Scudder knew how to handle them. The instant a renter cleared his stuff off the chair, Scudder would pounce, and before the customer could get to the sand bridge, both lounges and the umbrella would be next to the beach box. This let the hangers-on know that they were holding him up, and that if they insisted on taking the full time, it would be inconvenient for Scudder. Usually the guilt would move them out; sometimes it didn't.

Today everybody seemed to get the message, and he could have been out of there by four. However, after he was alone, he didn't feel like leaving. Billy Boy was in town until the weekend, and he had no obligations. He just sat down and reveled in his cleverness

These people were lambs waiting for the slaughter, he thought. *Hell, I'll own this beach before long.*

As he let his mind run, his eyes roamed over the

beach, and he noted with approval the approach of a very well-put-together beach bunny. Maybe five-foot-four or five-foot-five, long blonde hair, string bikini very well filled. He guessed twenty-four or so. As he watched, he felt a stirring deep inside, and it dawned on him that there had been something missing from his life that couldn't be denied. He glanced quickly around; then chuckled to himself at the thought. A little too early for what he wanted to do. Too much light. Too many people around. But that didn't stop him from trying something a bit more civilized, only just a bit.

"Yo, Sugarbritches," he turned on the charm. "Whatcha doing walkin' down the beach all by yourself?"

Normally this approach didn't even merit a stutter step by the object of his attention, but this time the woman turned and headed toward him. As she approached, he could see bright blue eyes, a cute turned up nose, and a healthy splash of freckles.

She's fuckin' beautiful. Star quality. Even Scudder wondered why she'd taken the bait. *Must have misunderstood me. What the hell, though.* "Sugar, you're about the cutest thing I ever did see. I'll bet honey drips when you talk. What're you doin' all by yourself?"

"Well yo, yourself. I'm down here by myself 'cause there ain't nobody with me, for your information," she replied, after the fashion of Scarlett O'Hara. Perhaps a lower class Scarlett, but that suited Scudder just fine. Scudder's social standing and education didn't really qualify him to make the subtle distinctions. He just knew she wasn't speakin' Yankee, and he didn't really care if she was speakin' Eskimo, as long as he could understand her.

"Well, where you from, darlin'? I'd be happy to help you in any way you might need helpin'," Scudder drooled.

"Well, I'm from Georgia, Jefferson City," she explained. "I'll bet you don't even know where that is."

"I might and I might not," Scudder covered his lack of geographical knowledge. "What're you doin' here?"

With a smile and a wink that caused Scudder to shudder somewhere in the vicinity of his groin, she said, "Lookin' for a good time."

After a pause, and what Scudder hoped wasn't an audible gulp, he continued, "I'm your man, darlin'. You come to the right place. Wanna go upstairs to my condo for a drink?"

"Hey, slow down, sugar. Let's just don't jump naked. A girl needs to know some things," she cooed. "Like what's your name?"

"Oh, yeah. My name's Scudder, and I'm about the best thing on this beach," he backpedaled, hoping he hadn't screwed this up. "So, hey. Why don't you and me go out and boogie tonight, and then maybe you'll feel more comfortable? Eh, what's your name?" That seemed like such a dumb question after he had just invited her for a roll in the sack.

"Why, my name's Kimberly. Kimberly Carter. And I just love to dance. I love to dance more than anything. Well, just about anything," she said with a look.

Aw right! Scudder exulted silently, having thought he'd blown it for sure. "OK, then, Miss Kimberly Carter, whadaya say we go to the Florabama and get down with some country music and cold beer?"

This seemed satisfactory, and they agreed they'd meet at Peg Leg's for a quick one around eight, and head to the Florabama from there.

The Florabama was named by someone with a practical streak because it happened to straddle the border between Florida and Alabama. A patron could literally order a beer in Florida, take two steps, and drink it in Alabama. Or for the dancer, do the interstate two-step. The club, with nothing between it and the gulf but sand, was immortalized by Jimmy Buffett, and was basically a beach honky-tonk that specialized in country music and rednecks; the kind of place you might think a person would go to get his ass kicked. However, the rowdier customers were kept in check, and the beer was cold. It was Scudder's kind of place.

Scudder didn't recall ever having a real date, and he wasn't quite sure about protocol, but he slipped into his best pair of jeans and only clean shirt, and after securing the OK from Billy Boy to use his beach car, went over to Peg Leg's to wait. After a few cold ones, he wasn't nearly as nervous as he had been, but even the alcohol didn't help much when Kimberly sashayed through the front door.

She was still beautiful, of course, but more so with her hair up and with makeup on. She was wearing one of those black things that look like one piece of material painted on, from just barely covering her boobs to about two inches passed her bum. Miss Kimberly had the figure for it.

Peg Leg's, normally a noisy, uproarious place, fell silent. Hell, it seemed like even the jukebox stopped. Every eye, whether reflecting jealousy or outright lust, went to Kimberly, and Scudder thought, *Here's where she gets snatched by some rich stud.* But as soon as she located Scudder, the rest of the people might as well have vanished, and she latched onto Scudder like a long lost lover.

Scudder, not being much of a lady's man, wasn't usually much good with conversation, but Kimberly made it easy. The whole evening went like that, not counting when they walked into the Florabama and there was an awkward pause by the band. They danced and drank, and drank and danced. In between times, Kimberly kept the conversation going smoothly. Scudder skipped the part about prison, but she seemed to be interested in anything Scudder had to say.

Finally, as they headed the car back across the Florida line, Kimberly moved Scudder's free hand between her legs as she thrust her tongue in his ear, almost causing a terrible accident as Scudder slid sideways off the highway. Getting breathlessly back on the highway, he shortly turned off on a road that led to a beach mostly used by amorous teens. Before Scudder could get the gearshift in "Park," Kimberly had doffed the dress, leaving her lusciously stark-raving naked, and had unzipped Scudder's pants.

From that point, it was pretty much a matter of Scudder trying to hang on. He had never experienced such passion. She did things to him that he'd never even imagined. As she maneuvered their bodies into yet another sort of embrace, Scudder gave up.

"I can't," he said. "I'm just out of gas. I wish I could, but there's just none left," he explained, feeling like some kind of inadequate sissy. Of course, it didn't help that she seemed to have just gotten her second wind.

Kimberly turned her head to the side without losing eye contact, as if to say *I thought you were the kind of man for me, but I guess not*. Then she whispered, "Well, I guess I'd better get dressed. Would you turn around?"

Scudder sheepishly complied, basically wishing he was dead. *Why, after all we've just been through, do I have to turn around?* he wondered, as he felt a cold hard object at the base of his skull. He never heard the two muted pops of the Beretta .22 automatic equipped with a silencer. He had gotten his wish.

Kimberly moved Scudder's lifeless body to the trunk, and quickly changed into a pair of cut-off shorts and a sweatshirt, leaving her party duds and blonde wig with Scudder. Per plan, she drove along Gulf Beach Highway to an isolated spot where Perdido Key meets the intracoastal waterway. As she drove, she removed the pancake makeup used to alter her appearance, and by the time she reached the water, no one would recognize her as the showstopper at Peg Leg's. Now she was just another attractive middle-aged snowbird who spent time at Pensacola Beach, not well known, but not unknown.

Checking for unwanted intruders that she knew

wouldn't be there at this time of night, she flashed the pre-arranged signal to beckon her cohorts. Shortly, a shallow-draft, high-powered boat arrived into which she entrusted the now-stiff body from the trunk. Percy Meriweather VanAlstine was going for a final swim in the Gulf of Mexico where he would never be found. William Turman would find his car in his garage, right where he left it, and after a brief period, no one on the island, except maybe Billy Boy, would even remember Scudder had ever been there.

"People don't talk about him no more. It happened just a week ago. People get by and people get high. On the island, they come and they go." Kimberly modified a tune by Jimmy Buffett, as she drove east toward Pensacola Beach thinking about the evening and singing.

Of course, her name wasn't Kimberly anything. It was Janie Jordan, and she had always been bent. She realized that most women weren't professional killers who liked to fuck their target before they killed them. Obviously, she chuckled to herself, there were very few professional killers. Some aspired to the profession, but most were stupid, and made their first contract with an undercover cop. End of career.

Janie supposed that her total lack of conscience and, really, contempt for her fellow human beings, had something to do with her father, who liked to beat her until she was about thirteen, when he began to use her for his sexual plaything. Fortunately, Janie had been smart and pretty, which got her a one-way ticket away from her father with a traveling criminal of her choosing. She'd learned a lot from him.

Now she was a member of a very elite club. She was difficult to locate, expensive to hire, but never made a mess of things or got caught. Most of her targets simply disappeared, and her clients were always satisfied. At least, she assumed they were satisfied. She got her money up front, and the client never knew anything about her, or how the contract would be executed. They just knew it would, soon and inevitably.

In between engagements, so to speak, she was ostensibly a writer. One of her books had even been published with some critical acclaim. It was a comedy, a farce. She liked that. It fit with her concept of how things were. Now she would submerge into her beach artist existence, until the next engagement.

Chapter VII

Slidell Goodbee sat in his squad car in the parking lot overlooking Casino Beach. The summer heat was now starting to charbroil the island as the humidity rose. It was Florida summer getting cranked. Later in the day, he knew that the atmosphere would become saturated, and it would rain somewhere near for a short time before nightfall. That would cool things off for the dark hours, and the whole thing would start over again with the dawn. Hey, it was summer. That's what happened in summer, and, as he sat watching, he was comfortable. He was used to the heat, there was a good wind blowing off the gulf, and it beat the hell out of sitting in an air conditioned office behind a stack of paperwork.

Being the duly elected sheriff, it wasn't necessary for Slidell to take a turn on patrol, but he liked to get out, and he felt that shouldering a share of the grunt work built office morale. He wasn't at Casino Beach to check on anything in particular; he was there to provide presence. If trouble was going to start, this would be the place. This was where the younger, more unruly, crowd came to "beach," and when you added a little alcohol to testosterone, sometimes things just happened. Also, some of the shadier elements liked to do a little dope with their sunshine, and if someone had the guts to bring the offender to his attention, he was sure going to remove the problem.

But now, as he looked at nothing specific, except an occasional well-endowed and underdressed beach bunny, he was thinking about the torched beach box. The Dallas County Sheriff's Office had been cooperative in establishing identity for the two victims. They had been here on a little three-day R&R, and were out for a moonlight stroll when the thing blew. Just innocents in the wrong place. Two minutes either way, and they would've been witnesses to a spectacular event, instead of dead. It was occurrences like that that made him wonder about why things happened as they did. Maybe the Bible thumps had the answer. God had other plans for those two. Otherwise, the sheer randomness was scary. But for the pebble the kid threw on the road, the horse wouldn't have stumbled and thrown the general, who then couldn't direct the attack which changed the outcome of the war that led to the enslavement of the race of people who would have discovered a cure for cancer as freemen, he mused. Stuff like that made him dizzy, and a little apprehensive.

So he did his best to ignore the whole thing, moving to potentially more productive areas, like who torched the box. Forensics hadn't come up with anything, except that the fire wasn't just a fire. There had been accelerants used, but what they found traces of were as common as dirt. There couldn't have been enough ingredients that their purchase would have attracted anyone's attention. There were no fragments that could be traced. What encased the lethal mixture was apparently consumed by the blast. The two victims were just too close.

That left him with suspects, people who might have had a motive. Scudder VanAlstine and Ernie Brown were the only ones he knew of who might profit from the crime. Scudder stood to make some extra money with his competitor out of the way, at least temporarily. Ernie might be collecting insurance. He'd take a closer look at Ernie; insurance proceeds would be easy enough to trace. He hadn't seen Scudder around for a while, which in itself was kind of suspicious. Maybe Billy Boy knew something about that. He didn't think the money involved was enough for murder, but whoever did it probably didn't plan on the Dallas couple being there. It wouldn't support a murder charge, but maybe manslaughter, in addition to arson and fraud.

*****

About a mile down the island as the sun moves, Ernie Brown was sitting comfortably back on his haunches, eying the new guy who was working Scudder's place. In that position, Ernie didn't look like Grizzly Adams; he looked like a grizzly bear, a blond grizzly bear. Tanned to a rich dark brown, his bulk and wooliness immediately brought to mind the nature scenes from TV. If he'd been scratching his back on an old tree, it would have been perfect.

He wasn't scratching his back, though, he was thinking about his gone beach box, and arriving at pretty much the same conclusions as Slidell – omitting himself as a suspect, of course. He had been wondering where Scudder had vanished to, and who this new guy was.

Ernie's insurance company was balking at paying for his loss, partly because he couldn't objectively substantiate the equipment stored inside, and partly because they suspected that he was the doer. They'd probably eventually pay for most of his loss, but in the meantime, he'd have to come up with some money or credit, or sit here and watch Scudder – and now the new guy – pig down his customers. Having changed from a man of peace to a more swashbuckling mode, he was also thinking about beating the truth out of Scudder VanAlstine, but that was going to be hard if Scudder didn't show up. But, in any case, it was time for action.

Lumbering down the beach, Ernie approached the new guy with all the delicacy his looks portended. "Hey, where's Scudder?"

The new guy, whom Ernie would have described as a skinny, pasty-faced wimp, turned and looked searchingly into Ernie's eyes, spreading his arms palms up, and answered slowly, "I'm afraid I have no knowledge of a person named Scudder, but perhaps I may be of assistance."

For a moment Ernie thought he had found David Carradine, reincarnated on the beach. But regrouping, he persisted. "Scudder's the guy who did what you're doing before you. I want to know where the son of a bitch is."

"Oh. I'm afraid I can't help you. I was employed only yesterday, and they said nothing of this Scudder. Perhaps he moved to another job," he monotoned. "I only thank God I was lucky enough to find this position. I asked no questions about a predecessor. It was enough that they should hire me."

Ernie opened his mouth to argue, but realized he had nothing to say. If the guy didn't know, he didn't know. Also, he had seen the real Kwai Chang in action, and he didn't want to be rolled down the beach. So, since he had his mouth open anyway, he introduced himself.

It turned out that the guy's name was Mark Albright and he'd been living at the Gospel House Church of God. He said he was given a lead for this job and applied. Ernie explained his position, and told him if he had any questions, feel free to ask. In the meantime, if Scudder showed up, let him know. Preparatory to Ernie going back to where he'd come from, they shook hands.

"See ya around," said Ernie.

"God bless you," said Mark.

Hmmm, thought Ernie, as he walked away.

*****

"Gospel House," answered the cheery voice. "God bless you, and how may I help you?"

"Eh, could I speak to... eh... Minister Tanner," requested Billy Boy, trying hard to sound like someone else.

"Hold please," came the reply.

"God bless you. Minister Tanner here."

"Farley, can you talk?" whispered Billy Boy.

"Turman, Turman, is that you?" Farley inquired

"Yes, yes, it's me," whispered Billy Boy with more urgency in his voice.

"Well, if you're alone, why are you whispering?" boomed Farley.

"Oh, yeah. I guess you're right." Billy Boy increased his volume. "Well, I guess you were right. Scudder seems to have disappeared. So I guess we better find someone else pretty quick." Pause.

"Don't worry about it, Turman. One of our boys is in place."

"But can we trust him? I mean, after all, he's with the church. I assume he's with the church," stuttered Billy Boy.

"It's OK. He doesn't look the part, but he knows the score. We can trust him to do the job," reassured Farley. "In fact, I think you'd like him. I don't think he drinks, but you might invite him up to your place for a... religious discussion." Pause.

"Well, if you're sure..." questioned Billy Boy.

"I'm sure," replied Farley, abruptly hanging up the phone. For a moment, he sat silently considering William

Turman. Finally he concluded, *if I didn't need him...*, and let the thought drop.

Billy Boy wasn't happy about the conversation either. There was something he couldn't quite put his finger on, but something was disturbing him.

Oh, well, he thought, *maybe I'll take Farley's advice.* Billy Boy wished he'd gotten the new guy's name.

Chapter VIII

If anybody had been awake at the Surf's Up, or walking down the beach directly in front of it, they would have noticed some majorly peculiar events going on around three in the morning. It was basically a seven-man operation; six on the wet team plus Albright. From out of the beach box, now managed by Mark during the day, snaked a long tube about one foot in diameter. It was colored white to match the color of the sand. Standing at the box itself was a man dressed in a black wet suit, as was each of the people involved. It was his job to monitor what amounted to a large suction device powerful enough to draw objects for a distance of up to one hundred yards, while separating the sand out and allowing water to drain away near the beach box.

Two other men in black were in the surf, just past the

small, gently breaking waves. It was one of those nights when the Gulf of Mexico resembled a large lake more than an ocean. Theirs was the most physically difficult job. They handled the business end of the vacuum, sucking debris and sand from the beach bottom. They were equipped with small air tanks, diving masks, and waterproof lights.

The remaining two outside participants were lookouts, posted fifty yards east and west from the beach box. Because it took some time to close down the operation, their function was to delay, permanently if necessary, any intruder who happened unexpectedly along the beach.

Finally, the good eye, so to speak, was posted on the roof of the Surf's Up. This roof access was conveniently gained through a trap door which had been misplaced during the original construction, and rediscovered when Billy Boy redid his condominium on the top floor of the building. This "eye in the sky" kept constant watch with night-vision binoculars for anything of interest, and particularly for any police vehicle that showed an inclination to slow near the Surf's Up. Each man, except the two in the surf, was equipped with a two-way radio. The entire setup could be totally concealed in the beach box in under five minutes.

To minimize the chances of detection, the operation was only conducted on overcast or moonless nights. Although larger swells would discourage the occasional all-night sports fishermen, anything much over a foot made it difficult for the guys in the water to handle the vacuum. However, in the darkness, the camouflage made the activities undetectable, absent special gear. The sound of the vacuum was minimal because it used an electric motor; any remaining machine noise was masked by the surf.

    For seven, to as many as fourteen, days a month, depending on conditions, the small task force would hit the beach between two-thirty and four-thirty in the morning. The go signal was when the waitstaff left Peg Leg's, and the shutdown time varied within thirty minutes, depending on sunrise. Occasionally, a couple would attempt to consummate a new-found relationship on the beach, but they were easily discouraged by the presence of unkempt men lurking in the shadows. The sheriff's deputies would investigate any cars parked along the road at a late hour, so the law unwittingly but effectively helped out by keeping the kids away.

    Not counting the select six, the beach box was the key. The equipment was understandably bulky, and had to be kept on site. The beach box was perfect. A night's catch could even be kept inside it for a few days, if the hoist couldn't be used to haul it up to Billy Boy's condo immediately after activities ceased.

    Clearly, since it was impossible to store the actual beach rental equipment inside the box, the concessionaire was an important player. He had to bring all the rental things in his van, and haul it out to the beach each day. Also, it was imperative that he keep everybody the hell out of the box when it wasn't locked up at night. An overly inquisitive or talkative person in this position wouldn't work out at all, and, like the late Scudder VanAlstine, he couldn't be attracting unnecessary attention to the area.

Of course, it was always possible that someone's curiosity would be aroused by the hauling of equipment from a van, but the beach setup was always in place or removed when the suspicion of the most obvious persons, other concessionaires, might be piqued. The casual observer wouldn't know, or would only think the equipment from the van was extra or replacement.

However, since its inception, the operation had gone smoothly, at least until Scudder came along. The use of a non-professional had been a mistake, but fortunately Farley had remedied it before it became costly. Now he had specially recruited a man and raised the pay. Mark understood the operation and stood, along with the others, to make a profit if it continued to be successful.

When Mark had appeared at the door of Gospel House, it was like a gift from heaven, in a manner of speaking. As with all new potential recruits, Farley had arranged through a friend at the Pensacola Police Department to have Mark run on N.C.I.C.. He wasn't actively looking for henchmen, but you couldn't be too careful. All these stories nowadays about men of God buggering anything that happened by the church had him on guard. Farley didn't want any negative attention drawn to his setup, especially attention of that nature. Nobody likes pedophiles, even born-again pedophiles.

It was with relief, then, that Farley discovered no sex offenses in Mark Albright's past. He, however, did discover a list of fraud and bunko charges that would make a gypsy blush.

Fortunately, no convictions. After making a few well-placed phone calls to contacts he had maintained from his former life, Farley established that Mark was a stand-up guy who could be trusted, as far as felons go.

It hadn't been necessary to explain that in 1559, Don Tristan de Luna had entrusted three schooners to return to Spain from Pensacola with the majority of his plunder from the New World, not to mention the plunder he had liberated from other pirate wannabes. Or that after proceeding east in the gulf from Pensacola Pass for less than a day, they had been smitten by one of the still-popular gulf hurricanes, which had driven them back from whence they came and splattered them right into what was now Pensacola Beach. The details of why Farley believed the booty of de Luna's three messengers was now embedded in the beach right in front of the Surf's Up Tower were likewise unimportant to Mark. Furthermore, it was of no import to Mark that a small, but learned, group of treasure hunters agreed with Farley.

It was pertinent to Mark that retrieving the treasure was highly illegal, which was why none of the other like-minded fortune seekers were involved. Not only was tearing up the sand, if you can tear up sand, around Pensacola Beach very politically incorrect, but also the U.S. Government and the Santa Rosa Island Authority deemed it a very serious matter. Furthermore, since Farley did not report income from the loot, and because he didn't wish to give the government its share, he would, if caught, be subject to even more penalties at the insistence of the United States, the State of Florida, and probably the local tax collectors.

Ever the one with an eye for ill-gotten gains, when Farley suggested that Mark might be included in a share of the loot, Mark immediately signed on as a member of Farley's villainous little group of soldiers of fortune. Farley, elated with his discovery, pronounced Mark the new beach box boy, not too long after poor Scudder received his final footlocker from Davy Jones.

Farley explained that it wasn't necessary that Mark know any of the names of the crew. This was true because he'd have no need to make contact with, or even see, them. Further, if things went suddenly sour, nobody could rat out anybody else for a place in the witness protection program. Only two of the people involved would know Mark, and those two were the only ones Mark would know. He obviously knew Farley, but after he left Gospel House, he was never to contact him directly. His contact for all purposes would be William Turman. Turman would make himself known to Mark, and they could develop their requisite cover.

As they parted, from Mark's perspective, Farley asked a curious question: "Say, Mark, you're not homophobic or anything, are you?"

Chapter IX

Rudolph Commins didn't smoke or drink, went to church most Sundays, and sent money home to his wife every payday like clockwork. Rudolph was stationed at N.A.S. Pensacola, training to fly the F14 Tomcat, and he took that opportunity and responsibility seriously. When he wasn't learning all he could cram down about being a Navy flyer, he was either asleep, calling home to check on his wife and kids, or working out. If Lieutenant Rudolph Commins had a flaw as a potential Naval aviator and a human being, it was that he suffered from periodic bouts of insomnia.

After a particularly difficult week of schools, he and his fellow trainees were rewarded with a twenty-four-hour pass. Because it wasn't really long enough for a trip home, Lieutenant Commins decided to use the time as it was intended. He rented a room at one of the cheaper beach motels, and prepared to spend some quality rack time.

Sometime after two in the early morning, Rudolph awoke, as in wide awake. After forcing his eyes shut and thinking relaxing thoughts for an hour, he gave it up and decided to go for a run on the beach. Maybe he could tire himself enough for sleep, he reasoned. In the back of his mind, he knew that plan had never worked before, but, what the hell, he had to do something other than just lay there.

"We got an intruder," said the eastern lookout man of the excavation team. The rest of the team knew what that meant. It meant cease activities, and get ready to shut down. If the intruder couldn't be stopped, they would have to move quickly.

Rudolph had finally gotten into the zone where the running seemed almost effortless and the endorphens, or whatever, kicked in. It had taken more time than usual; running in sand was a bitch. However, he had located the support of the hard sand next to the water, and now he was lost in trying to think through a flight simulator exercise he had screwed up the day before. From out of the shadows, a black-clad figure loomed immediately ahead, waving his arms and shouting something.

"Yo, hey! You can't go this way. We got some beach

construction. Go back," came the voice.

Rudolph had no reason to question the figure; he seemed to know what he was doing. So Rudolph turned back. But as he backtracked, he began to think. *That guy didn't have a badge or any identification. He didn't even say he was someone in authority. I'll bet he's just jackin' with me.*

If Rudolph had another flaw, it was the chip on his shoulder when it came to his race. *Screw him,* concluded Rudolph, *I'll just circle around that honky.* He then made an end run through the dunes, emerging behind the lookout.

"We got trouble." The radio crackled with the voice of the roof man. "Intruder has breached the perimeter. Repeat. Intruder has breached the perimeter. Shut down. Shut down."

Immediately, the box man began reeling in the vacuum hose, as the wet team moved toward the beach trying to facilitate the process. Both lookouts now converged on the beach box. Even with short notice, it looked like they could button up before the intruder could get close enough to see what was going on.

Almost in concert with the frustrated cry of the box man, the hose stopped. It was caught on a piece of driftwood, perhaps part of de Luna's old ships. There wouldn't be enough time now, and the lookouts closed faster.

Now Rudolph could recognize the flurry of activity

ahead, and began to discern shapes of people and some kind of long tube. It was then that he began to reconsider his decision to continue after being warned off.

Rudolph slowed to evaluate the situation, and heard the sound of footsteps approaching rapidly from behind. Relying on his natural athletic ability and strength, plus what he had learned in basic training, he turned to meet the sounds closing from behind. Immediately, he recognized the shape of the extended handgun, and dove to his left as the soundless spit of fire caused sand to blast up into his face. Then diving toward the attacker and to the right, Rudolph managed to grab the weapon as it spit again. This time he felt as if a sharp blow had hit his right knee. The good news was the gunman had over-corrected, and now he had his hand on the gun with his thumb wedged in front of the hammer.

Physically, even wounded, there was no contest. Rudolph easily wrenched the gun away from his attacker, and began pummeling him, mostly because the adrenaline was now flowing freely. As he was beginning to withdraw from the downed man, he felt a sharp blow to his upper back, followed by intense pain. Then again. Then nothing.

The wet team was a bunch of thieves and adventurers, not professional killers. When they discussed the operation with Farley, everybody had hinted darkly at what must be done if they were discovered, but no one had actually made a plan. Now they were standing on a public beach at four o'clock in the morning with a dead guy, and nobody knew what exactly to do with him. Too soon, beachcombers would begin their dawn scrounging.

They at first discussed deferring their problem by placing the corpse in the beach box for later disposal, but decided the hot sun could create real difficulties before it could be removed. However, it was clear that the main concern was that the body could not be found anywhere near the Surf's Up.

Then one of the six hit on the perfect plan. They would winch the body up to the roof, and ultimately into Billy Boy's condo, in the same manner they secreted their nightly discoveries. How clever this was, they mused collectively, at least until they abruptly discovered that the former Rudolph Commins weighed much more than their nightly booty. This epiphany occurred about three-quarters of the way up, when the chain securing the basket to the rope broke on one side. This caused the late lieutenant to swing into the building, and crash through a window on the tenth floor.

The initial awe changed to panic, which then began to subside as no light came on in the violated condo. Only the sound of the surf and the tinkle of falling glass could be heard. Vain hope was shattered, however, as a light suddenly illuminated the jagged edges of the window, and was immediately followed by a scream heard easily on Perdido Key. Like so many black cats in an alley, with the light they vanished.

*****

Slidell Goodbee had finally gotten his evening with Daphne Fairhope: "Blues on the Beach" – a beach concert courtesy of Steve Gunter and company – followed by a quiet dinner at Chan's, upstairs. Of course, being the sheriff, Slidell couldn't get wild with the wine, but Daphne had been intoxicating enough. Her light brown hair, streaked with blonde highlights and worn casually in a ponytail, was offset deliciously by natural good looks and the rich brown tan she had clearly spent many hours perfecting. A strapless pastel summer dress, clinging in all the right places to her lithe contours as she moved, created just the proper mystique to generate an urgency in Slidell to be alone with her.

As they dined, quietly discussing this and that, Slidell couldn't help but note that the candlelight accented the gold flecks in her brown eyes, making them appear to sparkle. Yes, Slidell was horny, and it didn't help that Daphne was drop-dead beautiful.

After the meal, they wandered down to the sand on Casino Beach, and strolled barefoot near the surf. Realizing the moonless overcast sky left little to see, Slidell maneuvered his willing partner back to his car and headed for his condo overlooking the sound. The night went according to plan.

At least, it went according to plan until five o'clock the next morning, when the startling ring of the bedside phone reluctantly roused a deeply satisfied and soundly sleeping Slidell.

"Goodbee. What?"

"Sheriff," whined his new dispatcher, "I hate to bother

you, but I think you need to get out to the Surf's Up Tower on the beach."

"I know where the Surf's Up is, Jasper," growled the groggy sheriff. "Just tell me what's the problem."

"Some black guy killed himself by jumping through this woman's window on the tenth floor," came the breathless response. Slidell wondered if Jasper was a druggie, as he assured him he was on the way and hung up the phone.

When Slidell arrived, he observed two of his patrol units parked under the marquee. The sun was just breaking the high cirrus clouds of dawn, and he was pleased to see that his deputies had not left their top racks flashing. No need causing a big scene if the guy's already dead. Bad for business, he thought.

He was greeted by one of his deputies at the front desk, and ushered up to unit #1020. The deputy at the unit door explained that it was owned by Steve and Jan Casper, who lived in Alabama, but who were now in residence. At this time, they were in the bedroom. Mrs. Casper was quite upset and her husband was trying to calm her down. Noting this, Slidell and his deputy passed by the kitchen into what Slidell took to be the living room.

The first thing that occurred to Slidell, as he took in the crime scene, was that the Caspers sure had a dynamite view when their picture window wasn't shattered. Clearly, as Jasper had said, something, presumably the body on the floor under the blanket, had come in through the window. Most of the broken glass now littered the living room floor. Moving to the window, Slidell noted that there was no visible means of entrance from the outside, not even a window ledge.

Slidell then undraped the corpse as his deputies turned away. These guys were not big city homicide cops. The body was clothed only in a pair of shorts and running shoes, and it had been pretty well cut up when it came through the window, if it did really come in that way. Looking closer, he found two small holes in the upper mid-back area. These did not look like punctures from shards of glass, and when he turned the body over, the substantially larger exit wounds confirmed Slidell's suspicion. He was going to have to get Pensacola P.D. involved here. However this guy got here, it didn't have anything to do with suicide. He needed forensics and an M.E..

Slidell told one of the deputies who to call and what to tell them, then knocked on the bedroom door before entering. Mrs. Casper had apparently calmed down enough to dress, as had her husband. From their perspective, there wasn't much to tell. They were awakened in the middle of the night by breaking glass, and when they went to investigate, they discovered the body just as it was now. It had seemed cold to just leave it there with nothing, so they had covered it with a blanket. End of story.

Slidell and the people from Pensacola P.D. would continue to gather evidence around the crime scene, and regroup later to compare notes. In the meantime, he would look around himself.

Of course, the best bet was that the Caspers had "done" Rudolph Commins, and concocted this story. Slidell knew his men would search the condo for a murder weapon and other evidence that might point to the Caspers. So, putting that aside, he began with the assumption that, even if it turned out that the dead could fly, the body had to have come in from above or below, from the roof or the beach.

There wasn't anything suspicious on the roof. Just a roof-access door that proclaimed to be locked, but wasn't. Anyone could have been up there, or not. There were several cigarette butts lying in a pattern that made it look like someone might have been up there smoking. By their relative age, apparently whoever smoked them was a regular. That seemed to add up to an employee who took his smoke breaks on the roof. But, just in case, he'd ask forensics to check them for fingerprints, if that could be done in this instance.

Downstairs, Slidell noted that the sand around the hotel looked like… well, sand. There was some broken glass that probably fell from the Caspers' window, but not enough to be the result of somebody jumping out. Besides, the dead guy was inside.

As he methodically expanded his search radius, he hit pay dirt, or pay sand in this case. A little down the beach to the east, he found stains in the sand that could have been blood. Of course, that could have belonged to a wounded surfer, but if it matched with the guy upstairs, then it might mean he met his end on the beach and for some reason was moved somehow to unit #1020.

    Curiouser and curiouser. He'd have to let this one percolate for a while. Maybe forensics and the M.E. would turn up something. For now, he'd tape off the areas, and hang around until the body was taken.

Chapter X

Honest Ernest Brown had managed to scrounge up enough cash and credit to come up with a slightly used complement of chairs and umbrellas, and had constructed a new beach box at the old site. He was now broke, and indebted to Annie the fence to the tune of five hundred dollars. So it was not surprising that he was busily putting out equipment early on the morning following the murder of Lieutenant Commins.

He had been thinking so hard about how long it would take to pay Annie back, as he was setting up his area, that he hadn't noticed all the hubbub going on at the Surf's Up. However, the cry of a particularly obnoxious seagull had turned his attention in the direction of the condos, and he wandered over to see what was going on.

The area was dotted with yellow crime-scene tape, and

uniformed deputies and other official-looking people were busily measuring, sampling, and looking hard at stuff near the condos. He recognized one deputy, an asshole named Atwood, who had frequently rousted Ernie in the old days, standing away from the general area of activity.

"Yo, Atwood! What cooks?"

"Well now, if it isn't Honest Ernest Brown," responded Atwood, turning in Ernie's direction. "And why would it be any of your business?"

"Just curious. First, my stuff gets torched, and now there's yellow tape all over the place next door," said Ernie. "Maybe we got a new hotbed of crime and violence."

"There's nothing here that concerns you. Unless you know something about some funny goings-on around here last night, go on about your business," ordered Atwood, pointing in the direction from which Ernie had come.

"Well, as a matter of fact, Atwood, some of the boys over at Bobby D's was talkin' the other night, and one of 'em had heard ol' Scudder VanAlstine braggin' as to how he'd eliminated some of his competition. Ol' boy said the way Scudder said it, sounded like he was talkin' about my beach box," explained Ernie.

"Sounds to me like a bunch of derelict beach bums drinkin' and swappin' lies," Atwood sneered.

"Whatever, Atwood. Take it for what it's worth. If it turns out to be important, and Slidell finds out you knew and didn't say nothin'..." Ernie let his voice trail off as he turned and headed back to work.

As Ernie moved in the direction of his equipment, he was thinking. *No wonder the crime rate's so high. Asshole cops think they're too smart to listen to what citizens have to tell 'em.*

Deputy Atwood was thinking that maybe it wouldn't hurt to pass this information on to the sheriff. It'd make him look good if it turned out to be something. If not, at least the sheriff would know he'd been paying attention.

*****

Considering the players in Farley's little band of blackhearts, it was really difficult to get them all together for any kind of conference. At the very best, nine guys assembled, with one being a known homosexual, would wind up with Farley being labeled a homosexual if someone spotted them. Of course, at worst, someone would somehow make the actual connection, and expose the whole sordid plot.

But he had done the best he could, figuring that eight guys, if they came individually, wouldn't cause notice in a casino. If they then slipped away from the slots, or whatever, they could individually go to a hotel room in the same building. If it was out of town, it would cut down on the possibility they'd be seen by someone they knew. The Biloxi Hotel Casino fit the bill perfectly, and that's why Farley, Billy Boy, and the wet team were now seated, as best the room would allow, in a discussion of the status of their scheme. Farley hadn't thought it necessary to include Mark; his end of the play wouldn't be affected.

Farley was summarizing. "I estimate that, to date, we've managed to extract one million dollars in gold doubloons and artifacts, and my best estimate is there's another fifty million waiting to be taken out. And waiting patiently, I hope, because now the law will be snooping around for who knows how long. How the hell did you guys allow this to happen?"

"We couldn't help it, Farley," ventured the lookout who had made initial contact. "I waved the guy off, and he looked like he was going away. He must've doubled back through the dunes. How can you figure a guy's gonna do something like that?"

To that they all nodded affirmation.

"You couldn't help it? You couldn't help it? What was the guy doing on top of the condos? Playing with himself?" blustered Farley.

To this there was dead silence.

Then, just before their ears began to ring, "I thought he was going back. I turned to look for other cars, and when I swept the area, I picked him up coming out of the dunes. Hell, it was just luck I spotted him before he was on top of the vacuum," said the roof watch guy.

"Yeah, that's real luck. We had to put the man down. You drop him through somebody's window, and we're real lucky," mocked Farley. "Some luck."

Despite his raving, Farley realized that what happened on the beach was just one of those Murphy's Law things that happen. But raising hell made him feel better. Everybody seemed to understand that at some level.

"OK." Farley paused. "We gotta shut it down. Let's hear some suggestions about time."

The suggestions ranged from two weeks to a conservative six months. Considering the risk/return, Farley went with one month, long enough for everyone to lose interest, but still enough time to take out some more stuff before the season ended, making their cover implausible.

"OK, gentlemen, we'll meet here one month from today to get cranking again. Same time, same M.O.," said Farley. "Now let's vamoose. On the ten minutes. You first, Turman.

"And for Christ's sake, try not to get busted for anything. We need you here in a month, not over in Starke," Farley instructed, as an afterthought.

*****

Kenny Goodfellow was an active member of the Gospel House Church of God, so, considering that the sect was rabidly anti-almost-anything-fun, but especially gambling, he almost wet his pants when Reverend Tanner strolled toward his table. If the reverend caught him playing roulette, he'd be forever banned from the church, and no telling what other horrible things he'd bring down on Kenny's head.

Farley had been heading for the door when he noticed that Billy Boy had lingered at the crap table, and he realized he'd forgotten to tell him something. Reasoning that a quick word now would avoid the necessity of contacting Billy Boy for a month, he quickly looked around and moved to Billy Boy's back. Not wanting to attract unnecessary attention, he gently placed his hand on Billy Boy's shoulder and whispered in his ear, "Make sure Mark knows the deal."

Kenny Goodfellow used Farley's distraction to scoot out of there, thanking God for his intervention, and promising to do some good deed in repayment. It wasn't until he was halfway to Pensacola that it dawned on him: *What was the reverend doing in a gambling casino nuzzling a known homosexual?*

*****

Slidell sat at his desk facing his two top deputies, men who had proven their ability to solve a crime. On the desktop were two folders: one from the M.E. and the other from the crime lab.

"So," Slidell was saying, "this is what we've got. Forensics says the victim's blood and the blood we found on the beach match. Forensics also says they got some partial prints on the cigarettes on the roof, and some more on the ledge. The ones from the ledge were pretty good. The prints on the cigarette butts weren't. Maybe a match, but maybe not. Nothing worthwhile in court. For what it's worth, forensics confirmed the body came from outside the window.

"The M.E. says the victim died of two gunshot wounds to the back, probably from a nine millimeter. He says the glass wounds were probably inflicted *post mortem*, but in any case, wouldn't have resulted in death. He says the time of death was around four in the morning.

"We have two people in the unit where the dead guy was found. They say they know nothing about how he got there. The condo manager says the Caspers are who they say. He says he doesn't know them very well. They mostly keep to themselves. Right now we know of no connection with the dead guy and the Caspers.

"Under 'stuff that might be related,' we've got an exploding beach box in the immediate area that resulted in two deaths. In both cases, there's a local scumbag loosely connected to each individual crime, and maybe connected to both. Scudder VanAlstine worked the area where the latest body was found, which was immediately adjacent to the area of the beach box deaths. Scudder has not been seen recently, and Atwood tells me the rumor is that Scudder torched the box to eliminate competition. Ernie Brown, who may or may not have cleaned up his act, was the owner of the torched box.

"So what do you think?" Slidell concluded.

"Well, it seems clear that the dead guy was killed on the beach and moved to Unit #1020, and since there were no signs of him being shot out of a cannon, he had to come from above," reasoned the deputy on Slidell's left. "But even if he had five stories to fall, I don't think he could have gotten the angle to go through the window on the tenth floor, so that doesn't explain how he did get there."

"The only thing that makes any sense to me is that

someone was lowering him down the side of the building, and maybe deliberately swung him into the Caspers' unit. Maybe some kind of revenge thing," contributed the deputy on Slidell's right.

"Yeah, that might work, but why didn't the Caspers know who he was?" queried Slidell. "Revenge isn't very sweet if the recipient doesn't know what's going on."

Silence for a moment while the group turned this over in their minds.

"Of course, what if the Caspers are lying?" the second deputy suggested.

"Could be. You want to take that angle? Check out any relationship the Caspers may have had with the dead guy. First, I guess you're going to need to find out who the dead guy was, but that shouldn't be too hard. Someone's going to wonder what happened to him." Slidell made the assignment.

"Well, what if the dead guy ending up in the Caspers' unit was an accident? What if somebody was lowering him to the beach?" the first deputy brainstormed. "But that doesn't work. If they killed him on the beach, why were they putting him back? And how did they get him into the condo building, anyway? No, that doesn't make sense."

"Unless," put in Slidell, "he wasn't being lowered. He was being lifted."

It was one of those moments. They eyed each other, as if to say *Yeah!*

Finally, Deputy One did. "Yeah. They killed him on the beach, and had to get rid of the body. There's no place to put it, and it's getting light. So they decide to put it on the roof. Then, maybe, dispose of it later. As they're hauling him up, the rope breaks and imparts the angle to send him through the Caspers' window."

"OK, if that's the way it played out," said Slidell, "someone connected with the condos is also connected with the dead guy. You want to work on that angle?" He nodded at Deputy Two. "Once we know who the dead guy is, it'll make it a lot easier. What else?"

"Whoever did it wasn't playing. Says here," noted Deputy One, as he leafed through the M.E.'s report, "they found powder burns on the guy's back. Someone most definitely intended to kill him."

"What about Scudder and Ernie?" asked Deputy Two.

"I'm not sure," mused Slidell. "I'll take care of that. I also want to take another look at that roof. What else?"

Apparently the brainstorm had ended, so Slidell suggested they get moving and keep each other advised of anything they found out. They'd meet in a few days.

Chapter XI

Ernie Brown sat in the sand in front of his beach box staring out at the gulf. This was one of Ernie's favorite things to do after stowing all his beach equipment for the day. It allowed him to mellow out, collect his thoughts, and kind of put everything in order before he moved on to whatever lay ahead. He could also scope out the remaining beach bunnies wandering down the beach at sunset.

This day had been relatively clear and hot, as usual, but the gulf wasn't following suit. Normally such weather would result in a lake effect, during which time you could see why one of the nicknames for this place was the Emerald Coast. Today, however, despite clear conditions, the gulf looked a lot like the stormy North Atlantic, complete with big breakers rolling in from far out. At least, the breakers were big by gulf coast standards; people in California would probably scoff.

But fuck California, Ernie mused, off on a tangent. *If they liked California so much, they should stay there.*

No, somethin' cookin' out there somewhere beyond the horizon. Some kind of storm or something. Who knew, maybe a hurricane? Ernie hoped it wasn't a hurricane.

Erin and then Opal had come through in the same year after seventy or so years of good luck, with near misses or nothing even close, and the beach still hadn't recovered. The sand wasn't quite as white, and the tides weren't quite right. Opal must have stirred up a lot of sand, not just on the beach, but offshore, close enough to change the flow of things.

As he watched the locals pretend they were shootin' the curl on Wiamea, Ernie wondered why he'd never tried to surf himself. Maybe time. Maybe he was concerned about not being any good. On the other hand, he admitted to himself, it was probably an intestinal thing: no guts.

With a perverse twist on that last thought, he considered what had happened to the guy at the Surf's Up. Newspaper, somewhere on page three, said he'd been shot, but not much more.

That's curious, Ernie was thinking. *Usually a murder right here on the Emerald Coast would have gotten more press play.*

More to this picture than meets the eye, Ernie concluded, as he watched the sky turn pink over the Portside Villas and wandered off, almost unconsciously, in the direction of the Surf's Up. Why would someone kill a guy right on the beach in front of a high-rise condo in the middle of the night? Robbery sounded right. Maybe one of those chance meetings, "wrong place, wrong time" things. Pensacola Beach, at least at this end, wasn't exactly a place for dirtballs to congregate, but anybody could be anyplace at one time or another.

*****

Had Slidell Goodbee been aware that he and Ernie Brown were sharing a thought, he probably would have joined some sort of twelve-step program. But he wasn't aware of that. He was only vaguely aware that he was pointing his black-and-white in the direction of the home of Daphne Fairhope, which was a good thing. Daphne had a strong tendency to be mightily pissed when he was late, or failed to show at all, and didn't call. She understood that Slidell had a job that was important, and to which he was totally committed, but to her way of thinking, any damn fool could pick up a phone, especially one in his car.

Slidell wasn't thinking about shapely, seductive Daphne, or romance, or food, or anything in that order. He, like Ernie Brown, was thinking about the late Lieutenant Rudolph Commins, and he had more to work with than Ernie did.

Sure enough, it hadn't been too long before a "missing person" was filed by the Navy, indicating that one of their flight candidates was A.W.O.L.. Checking further, the deputy in charge had easily determined that Lieutenant Commins was that missing person, and that no one, not even his family, knew where he had been or why he was on Pensacola Beach. However, since some of his "civvies" were missing from his quarters, and none were found with the body, the deputy had assumed he was staying somewhere on the beach. Figuring a serviceman's pay, and armed with a picture, it hadn't been real tough to locate the beach motel where Commins had been staying.

That was the good news. The bad news was that the trail led nowhere. Everyone who knew him or served with him had nothing but praise for his character and dedication to duty. There was nothing among his clothes at the motel to suggest much of anything. Only that he hadn't been planning on staying long, about as long as a twenty-four-hour pass would allow. The only thing of significance was that everyone concerned said Commins was an avid runner. This was consistent with what he was wearing when found.

The Caspers were from Montgomery, Alabama, and spent about four months a year on the beach at Pensacola. They had only arrived the preceding weekend to begin their annual stay. As far as anyone knew, Commins had never been to Alabama, and he had only been at N.A.S. for a month before he was killed. No connection.

Slidell's other deputy had acquired a list of people who either owned a condo at the Surf's Up or who had stayed there within the last month, but so far hadn't turned up any connections to Lieutenant Commins, or any leads at all. But then, he hadn't had much time since the identity of Commins had been established.

Slidell had been waiting for his deputies to come up with a positive identification, and so hadn't done much. He had gone back to the condo to look around on the roof. The only thing he came up with were some scrape marks on the gulfside railing, and a second roof access by trapdoor. The property manager indicated that the unit under the trapdoor was owned by William Turman, but as far as he knew, the trapdoor had been sealed years ago.

Not really a lot to go on. If the body hadn't ended up in the Caspers' unit on the tenth floor, Slidell would have written this off as a random murder that would probably never be solved. But it wasn't his experience that impulse murderers, or even racial killers, would take time to move a body very far. The random lunatic's means of evasion was the lack of a motive or connection to the victim. It was therefore unnecessary to cover up the crime. Here, there was some connection or motive that would expose the killer; hence, the need to hide the body.

Nope, there was something out there they just hadn't found or thought of. Maybe the deputy would come up with something. In the meantime, it was good that Slidell had worked this out in his head. Daphne's driveway was coming up on the left, and it wouldn't do for Slidell to be distracted by the murder all evening. This was another thing that tended to agitate Daphne, her feeling being that there wasn't much need for her to be present if Slidell wasn't.

*****

"Goddamn shit!!!" screamed a wounded Ernie Brown, grabbing his foot and falling sideways into the sand.

As Ernie held his wounded foot and continued to regale unfortunate passersby and residents of the Surf's Up with an exotic and profane tirade against the gods of fate, Mark Albright made his way as fast as possible from his window perch in Billy Boy Turman's top floor condo to the epicenter of the rantings. Mark had been idly watching Ernie when he made contact with an object that Mark immediately recognized.

The source of Ernie's pain was a titanium handgrip, custom-made to attach to the sea vacuum. The making of the handgrip had been accomplished by a highly skilled metallurgist, which made it readily identifiable and easily traceable. It was also very valuable and almost essential to the treasure dig. Apparently, it had been mislaid in the prior night's confusion, news of which had been extracted piece by piece by Mark from Billy Boy Turman.

As Mark cleared the beach entrance, Ernie sat holding the object of his anguish, examining it in the manner one might regard a vile and evil serpent. Apparently deciding the hated object should perish in the murky depths, Ernie stood and took the pose of Troy Aikman, substituting the handgrip for a football. As his arm began to move forward, Mark smashed into the back of Ernie Brown with the courtesy of a defensive lineman, causing the handgrip to flutter harmlessly to the sand as Ernie bit the dust.

Following a rolling tumble accompanied by Mark Albright, Ernie Brown sat staring bumfuzzled in the general direction of Mark.

"What did you do that for?" queried Ernie, too bewildered to swear.

In his rush to the beach, Mark hadn't prepared a justification for his actions. "You were about to throw away my... eh... beach tool." Mark now sat cradling the handgrip.

"What the hell kind of beach tool is that?"

"It's eh... it's eh... well, it's none of your business," stammered Mark.

Ernie eyed the malicious object. What it looked like was a very large crescent wrench with an oversized and permanent bolt attachment. Kind of like a Gillette safety razor, but bent at the blade attachment end, waiting for the razor to be attached.

"I've never seen anything like that at the beach before." *Or anywhere else*, Ernie thought. "What do you use it for?"

"Well," Mark made ratcheting movements, "for lots of stuff. You know, to loosen stuff."

"Like what stuff, Mark? Looks like a snap-on handle to me," Ernie probed.

"I don't care what you think it is. It's my beach tool, and I don't have to explain it to you." With that, Mark turned and strode back to the Surf's Up.

Ernie fought off the impulse to follow Mark and choke him 'til his eyes bulged, and limped off on his sore toe instead.

Hours had passed since Mark had decided that a little freelancing was in order. Although Ernie didn't look particularly bright, Mark knew otherwise. It was unlikely that Ernie would ever figure out what the handgrip was used for; but if anyone ever found the vacuum, he might, or somebody might, figure it out, especially if Ernie began talking about the strange tool he'd seen. Maybe he should have let him chuck it, but he hadn't, and now it was irrevocably connected to him. Ernie was going to have to be eliminated.

Anyone who knew Ernie knew his afterwork ritual. Down to Bobby D's for a few cold ones, then pedal home. So unless it was raining too hard, at about nine-thirty every evening, you could find Ernie on his bicycle headed down Via de Luna Drive for home.

If someone ran over Ernie at a cross street on the bike path, people would assume it was a drunk hit-and-run accident. There weren't any streetlights, the beach was full of drunk tourists, and, if anybody examined the corpse, he'd have a hefty blood/alcohol ratio. No Ernie, no problem. Farley and Billy Boy would be proud. Showing a little initiative. These were the thoughts that ran through Mark's head as he sat on the darkened cross street, east of Bobby D's.

As Mark had feared, Ernie was indeed thinking of the strange tool and the even stranger behavior of Mark Albright as he pedaled toward home. Perhaps he had his father to thank ("Always look both ways when crossing an intersection") when he spied the rapidly accelerating car coming right for him with its lights off. Ernie jammed the brakes hard and laid the bike on its side, rolling immediately away from the oncoming car.

Thank God I cheaped out on the toe clips, he thought. The bike was demolished, as he would have been were he a split-second slower. "Drink Guinness for strength," he muttered under his breath.

Of course, it was too dark to get a license number. But the car looked familiar, and considering the events of the afternoon, he knew who it was. He couldn't prove it in court, but then, he wasn't a lawyer.

Chapter XII

The Escambia County Sheriff's substation was a stucco affair sitting about rock-throwing distance from the gulf on Casino Beach near the only intersection of Fort Pickens Road and Via de Luna Drive. The idea was to make law enforcement high profile in the place where trouble would start, if it was going to start. The substation consisted of two offices, a holding tank, and a reception room, where Ernie now sat waiting for Slidell Goodbee at eight o'clock in the morning. He had specifically requested Goodbee because Ernie figured he was the only one in the sheriff's department who might take him seriously, and, considering his history, that was a long shot.

The prior night had been sleepless, at least until around three or four o'clock, when he must have dozed off. He knew he had eventually slept because the alarm woke him much too early. Regardless of what he did about the attempt on his life, he had to get his beach rigs set up before his customers decided it was sun time.

After the car assassin had sped away, Ernie had been in a mild form of shock. It wasn't every day that someone decided to run him down, and the experience had the immediate quality of unreality. Despite the fact that he was having trouble accepting that it had happened, he picked up his bike and moved in the direction of home. It was during this trip that he discovered that he had not escaped unscathed. In fact, his left side was a mass of scrapes and sore places which would become obvious dings on the morrow.

By the time he had limped home, showered, and cleaned his wounds, Ernie began to accept the fact that Mark Albright had tried to kill him, and the more he thought about it, the more he wanted to return the favor. Around midnight, with the help of a few shots of tequila, he convinced himself that he was ready for sleep. This was wrong.

First, he replayed the incident in his head. Then he fantasized what he would do to Mark. This varied from a straightforward beating at the Surf's Up to something more sinister where he cornered Mark in a dark parking lot. Then he considered that Mark, the weasel, would probably go to the sheriff and file charges against him for any attack he might carry out, which would put the ball in Ernie's court as far as the law was concerned. A cold calculated attack could not be justified as self-defense, and the result would be that he was arrested and convicted on the word of an attempted murderer.

Ernie envisioned his impassioned plea to the jury – notwithstanding that he wasn't a lawyer and wouldn't be saying anything to the jury – imploring them to do the right thing despite the law. Certainly a serious beating was justified by Mark's attempt on his life. But then he thought of the character issue. Mark the wholesome versus Ernie the derelict. Mark certainly wouldn't admit that he had tried to kill Ernie, so the jury would believe the beating was an unprovoked attack. That didn't play well.

Maybe he'd have to kill Mark; revenge with no consequences. But, in his heart, he knew he was no killer, at least not a cold blooded one. He'd have to use the system. Report the incident to the sheriff.

But then, in his nighttime musing, he saw Deputy Atwood smirking at him. Making light of his plight. Refusing to take the word of a former beach bum. Taking the report, and later depositing it in "file 13." No justice for Honest Ernest Brown in this criminal justice system.

And then the replay of the incident, but this time he got the license plate number and saw Mark behind the wheel. Still Atwood refused to believe him. Again justice would require taking matters into his own hands.

So the night went, until sometime when he must have dozed off. When he awoke, he realized he would at least have to give the system a try, at least for starters. And now here he sat waiting for Slidell Goodbee, hoping things would work out, but still knowing they probably wouldn't.

As the big hand made its way to the top, Deputy

Atwood announced, "Sheriff Goodbee will see you now, your honesty." Atwood thought himself a real comic.

Big yuk, asshole, Ernie thought, as he made his way back to Slidell's office.

"Well, Honest Ernest, what can we do for you?" asked the sheriff.

This is already starting out badly, thought Ernie, *but what the hell?* "Sheriff, I've got a problem."

As Ernie explained what happened, complete with the beach scene and the strange tool, the sheriff's sarcastic smile faded into attentive concern.

Maybe I was wrong. Maybe the law would help, thought Ernie.

Then Slidell asked the questions Ernie knew would come. "Did you get the license number? Did you see the driver? How do you know it was Mark Albright?"

"No. No." and "It was his car."

Then, "Do you suppose there could be two cars like that in Escambia County?"

"Of course there could, Sheriff." Ernie's heart sank with the realization that it really might not have been Mark. But that was on an intellectual level; his gut told him otherwise. *At least the sheriff gave me the courtesy of a full and serious hearing of my complaint,* Ernie thought, as the sheriff dismissed him.

"Tell you what I'll do. I'll do some checking. Maybe talk to Mark Albright, and get back to you."

Ernie thanked the sheriff and left, knowing he'd foreseen this conclusion. He just hadn't wanted to admit it to himself. He had nothing but a gut-level knowledge that Mark Albright was the guilty man. He just knew it, and he'd figure out a way to prove it, or maybe seek justice in his own way.

What Ernie couldn't know was that Slidell Goodbee believed every word Ernie had told him. This was just one more odd piece to a picture of something, and Slidell had no idea what that might be. He did know that he had three violent deaths and one attempt, all seemingly centered around the Surf's Up. Also a new piece: the weird tool.

What was it, mused Slidell, *that Ernie had discovered that was important enough to result in his death?*

Ernie's faith in law enforcement was renewed later that day when a deputy came to his house asking to take paint samples from his mangled bike. Unfortunately, there hadn't really been any. The automobile had crashed over the bike, not run into it. But maybe, Ernie speculated, there would be some damage to the car nevertheless.

Slidell was a bit ahead on that idea. He had made plans to personally go to the Surf's Up to talk to Mark Albright, and while he was there, take a look at Mark's car.

When Slidell arrived around noon, he found Albright sitting contentedly under a beach umbrella overseeing his operation. As he approached, he noted another person, who could have been William Turman, make a hasty exit. He had no idea what William Turman might have looked like in a bathing suit. In fact, he was glad he had never speculated about the subject, but regardless, he couldn't say for sure whether it was Turman or not.

Albright seemed not to notice the sheriff until he was almost on top of him, and then jumped to his feet.

"Hello, Sheriff. How can I help you?" Mark said unctuously.

Slidell noted that Mark didn't seem very surprised by the visit, considering that he'd never had reason to talk to Mark in his life. "Mark Albright?" Slidell inquired.

Mark nodded.

"I'd like to ask you a few questions, if you have time."

Clearly Mark had time, and said he'd be happy to assist in any way he could.

It sounded like a solid citizen response, but a little too much so. Most people were a bit wary in dealing with law enforcement. "Would you mind telling me where you were around nine o'clock last night?"

"Well, I'd really rather not, Sheriff, unless it's absolutely necessary. It's kind of a delicate matter," Mark hedged, looking away while answering.

"Take my word for it, Mr. Albright. It's absolutely necessary," intoned Slidell in his best cop tone.

"If you must know, I was in the company of Mr. William Turman, right here at the condo. Mr. Turman is a lawyer, you know," said Mark.

Ah, the veiled threat, thought Slidell. "Will he confirm that?" followed Slidell, hoping he might be able to catch Mark in a lie if he moved quickly. "Is he here now?"

"He might be busy. You know how lawyers are, but, yes, I believe he is here now," again holding up the talisman, but otherwise smooth as glass. Finally, Mark asked the question he should have asked first: "Why do you want to know where I was at nine o'clock?"

Slidell could have given him some mumbo-jumbo answer, but he was presumably innocent at this point, and if he wasn't, he knew damn well why. So Slidell explained that a car similar to his had been involved in a hit-and-run. He thanked Mark for his time, and departed in the direction of the Surf's Up to find Billy Boy Turman. He knew the unit number.

As he moved into the lobby, he admitted to himself that if Mark Albright was the doer, he was pretty smooth. Maybe Ernie had been wrong. However, he'd checked Albright's car before talking to him, and there was some damage in the area where the bike would have been hit. However, that type of damage was just as likely to have been done by a pothole going into Peg Leg Pete's.

Being suspicious by nature, and made more so by profession, Slidell delayed several seconds before boarding the elevator. Then he glanced around the corner toward the beach. Darned if Mark Albright wasn't on the pool phone, and if Slidell had been a gambling man, he'd have bet a week's salary he knew who was on the other end.

*****

"Billy Boy? Sheriff Goodbee is on his way up to see you. Tell him we were together all night from around six-thirty. It's vitally important to the operation that I have an alibi for last night. I'll explain later. It has to do with the tool I was going to tell you about." Mark hung up.

*****

Slidell knew that he was now wasting his time going to see Turman, but he'd go ahead and play it out.

As the elevator ascended, he marveled at the guts move he had just seen Mark Albright make. That man was dangerous; he'd have to remember that.

The interview was fairly brief. Knowing Turman's orientation, he didn't get into what they were doing from six-thirty until morning, but Turman backed Albright's play to the hilt.

That in itself meant something. Turman, even if he was gay, was still a respected member of the Pensacola Bar, and he had just lied like a rug to cover the tracks of a beach vendor. It was either true love or something a little more sinister. The latter, Slidell strongly suspected. But for now he just had a handful of supposition.

It did seem likely that Albright had tried to kill Ernie, and maybe was the hitter on Commins. Slidell would have to hope that his deputy could establish some connection between Commins and the Surf's Up, and that something else would break, too. It was nice that Albright and Turman had moved themselves front and center as likely connections. Slowly, slowly, but moving somewhere.

Chapter XIII

At six-thirty, when Mark really did go up to Billy Boy Turman's condo, he was greeted by both Turman and Farley Tanner. It had been quite a gamble for Tanner to come to Turman's unit, but when Billy Boy explained the stakes, Farley assumed that risk. On being admitted, Mark immediately noted the chill in Billy Boy and the menace emanating from Farley.

"Son, we don't need no freelancin' amateurs messin' 'round here," growled Farley before Mark could find a seat. "You have any idea how bad you fucked up?"

"Mr. Tanner, the guy was nosing around and found the vacuum tool someone left on the beach. We had to do something. If the wrong person got ahold of the tool, they might have figured out what was going on," pleaded Mark.

"So without talkin' to nobody, you decided the best way to take care of the situation was to whack him?" Farley's voice dripped with sarcasm. "And you come up with some fool plan that doesn't even work? And the next thing we know, Slidell Goodbee is snooping around you. So you do the right thing, and involve Turman. Right? Clever boy. Now, instead of a problem we might have down the road, we've got a for-sure problem, right now. Me and Turman got to decide what to do about that problem, clever boy. Maybe you'll share some of your cleverness with us."

Mark had been looking at the floor, doing his best penitent sinner imitation, but now he realized that alone wouldn't cut it. He also understood he might be the next MIA, if he didn't come up with something good. So he did. "Maybe we can scare Goodbee off."

Farley rolled his eyes to the ceiling.

"No, now listen just a minute," interjected Mark before either could attack his developing scheme. "Not so much scare as finesse. See, maybe if Goodbee thought he was meddling in some federal stuff, he'd back off." He paused to let that sink in. Also to figure out what he'd say next. To his relief, Farley seemed to be considering his plan.

"FBI's too close; he could check. Maybe CIA?" mused Farley.

"Yeah." Mark almost followed with: that's the ticket, but resisted. After all, this little gamble was probably for his life. "Maybe a late night call with a not-so-veiled threat of what could happen if locals mess with the big dogs?"

"Might work," said Farley. "Whadaya think, Turman?"

"Well, Goodbee is just a jerkwater sheriff. I never heard he was overly bright. Dedicated? Yes, but that can cut both ways. 'Dedicated' may be to the overall good of the order, as opposed to just his own bailiwick." Billy Boy seemed to be thinking out loud. "Especially since we don't have an alternate plan, it couldn't hurt. He already knows something's going on. What would it hurt if he thinks the CIA is behind it? Best scenario: he goes away and takes his deputies. Worst scenario: he continues to investigate, which he will do even if we don't do anything. I think we should go with it," he concluded, thinking that, in addition, whatever happened with the CIA thing, it would be better than another execution. One of his beach boys was enough.

Farley thought for a moment, seeming to weigh alternatives, then said, "OK, let's do it. Mark, you're out of this play. I'll handle it. You keep on doing what you've been doing. But no more murder attempts," he added quickly. "In fact, no anything out of the ordinary, without checking with Turman first. Understood?" he finished with a challenging glare.

"Whatever you say, Mr. Tanner." Mark inwardly relaxed. He knew damn well what the unmentioned alternative included, the one Billy Boy didn't mention and Tanner was weighing so carefully. He knew he was on what a person might characterize as terminal probation. Mark took his leave, already thinking what he might do to redeem himself. Something really good. He'd have to think about it.

As Mark left the condo, Farley was saying, "There's too

good a chance that Goodbee might know one of our voices, or identify it later, if he doesn't know it now. I'll get one of the team to make the call; fill him in on the deal, and what to say. How do you feel about ordering pizza?" he shifted subjects. "Can't leave now; too early. Maybe later I can get the hell out without being recognized."

With a mixture of euphoria for creatively wiggling out of a sticky situation, and perplexity from considering what he might come up with to get back in Farley's good graces, Mark moved through the deep purple that now descended on Santa Rosa Island. Probably his mental state was what caused him to miss the bear-like figure lurking near the truck parked next to his car.

Ever since the attempt on his life, Ernie had felt ill used. Violated was a better description. Being a manly kind of man, he had never understood what all the hubbub was about with female rape victims. Sure, he understood the violent ones, where the woman was beaten or cut or just snatched off the street or degraded, but not the variety where the guy just used his physical superiority to advance beyond the "no." After all, it wasn't like the guy used it all up, or irreparably damaged the goods, and the sex act was the sex act. After all was said and done, it had to feel good to the woman, too.

Now he thought he understood. He wasn't damaged, just shaken; and not really inconvenienced – not counting the bike. But somebody had impinged on a zone that was uniquely his, without his permission. Furthermore, that same person was now walking around with impunity. If Albright had just been punished, Ernie thought he'd feel a lot better about the whole thing, but he hadn't been. Albright had tried to kill him, take all he had or ever would have, and just walked off whistling a happy tune, so to speak. It made matters worse to see the skinny little fuck sitting under his umbrella, going about his business as if nothing had happened.

These thoughts had already caused one sleepless night, and had made an otherwise beautiful day unpleasant. As Ernie sat stewing beside his beach rigs, he arrived at a conclusion: it was a matter of taking his own vengeance or going crazy.

He had opted for the former. The key to his decision was the realization that he could do something short of maiming, and the worst that could happen was a misdemeanor. Two, he reasoned, could play the same game. Moreover, if Albright couldn't identify him, how could the law prosecute? Let Albright go to the cops, and tell them he thought it was Ernie Brown, but he couldn't identify him. *Ha!*

Initially, Ernie thought he would blacken his face, don black clothes, and attack ninja style, but then he thought better of it. Probably most people on the beach would be suspicious if they saw a large ninja creeping around. Besides, it wasn't necessary that he fool Mark. Regardless of what he looked like, Mark would know, and that was the good news and the bad news. So he decided to wear a Sylvester P. Pussycat Halloween mask. He could put that on quickly, and discard it just as quickly.

As things turned out, Ernie could have gone naked. No one was in the parking lot, and Mark didn't even notice him, but he donned his disguise anyway. "Ehhh, what's up, Doc?" said Ernie, trying to be cute, but confusing the trademark line, as he closed on Mark.

Mark turned distractedly and retorted, "You mean 'sufferin' succotash,' don't you, bub?"

"Fuck you," said Ernie, as he smashed a giant right fist into Mark's right cheek. It was the old two-hit fight: Ernie hit Mark, and Mark hit the ground. Lights out.

*****

Slidell Goodbee had invested in two pounds of fresh gulf shrimp from the Fish Peddler and a bottle of chardonnay from America, as the island locals referred to mainland Pensacola. It wasn't that the beach didn't have good wine. It was just that whatever you bought, it was at beach prices: high.

He and Daphne Fairhope had dined inelegantly but well, and, after sipping the remaining wine on Slidell's balcony overlooking the sound, retired to the boudoir. His investment had paid off, and he was up to his ears in fine southern womanhood when the phone rang. Truly this was the moment of truth, and duty won out.

"Yes," Slidell groaned, "Sheriff Goodbee."

"Goodbee," the muffled voice said, "you're gettin' into stuff that doesn't pertain to you."

Slidell's first thought was that Daphne had a husband she hadn't told him about. "Who is this? Whadaya talkin' about?"

"Let's just say I work for your uncle, and I'm talkin' about that business at the Surf's Up." Pause. "There's more goin' down than you know, Sheriff, and you're about to screw it up. Too much time has been put into this operation to let anyone screw it up. This is stuff that's way out of your league. I speak for your uncle himself, and he says to tell you it's a matter of highest national priority. We're takin' jurisdiction. Do you understand?"

"No, I don't understand," fumed Slidell. "If you're trying to tell me you're a fed, you can deliver that message through channels."

"Our agency," the voice confided, emphasizing the word *agency*, "doesn't go through the normal channels. We're, how'd you say, covert. Let me put it this way: sometimes, in the interest of national security, people disappear when they get involved where they shouldn't. Do your government and yourself a favor. Back off."

The phone went dead.

Unfortunately, so had he, and so had Daphne.

Much later that night, while Daphne slept soundly beside him, Slidell wondered what exactly was going on. He had told Daphne that the phone call was from a confidential informant, so he couldn't tell her what was said. That seemed to satisfy her, intellectually that is. They had made love, but the prior intensity was gone. It was still good, just not fantastic.

Clearly, the voice on the phone was telling him he was CIA. Slidell didn't know much about "the agency" – maybe that's the way they did business. But, still in all, it was a peculiar way to get things done. Surely one government agency could go through another to get messages across to local law enforcement. Why not simply have a representative from the State Department or the FBI pay him a call at the office?

On the other hand, it was rumored that the FBI and the CIA didn't work well together, and maybe they thought a call from the State Department might draw too much attention to a covert operation. But why all the BS? Why not just call and say, "This is the CIA and you're interfering with one of our operations. Stop and we'll fill you in later, or just stop 'cause we said so." Well, maybe that wouldn't work well either, but the threat of "disappearance" was a little strong, even for what he'd heard of the CIA. No, something wasn't right here. But, nevertheless, he'd try to check it out the next day.

*****

Slidell was still thinking about the phone call when he eased the black-and-white into his spot marked "SHERIFF ONLY. THIS MEANS YOU TOO." Although he had decided he'd just call Langley directly, and was on his way to do just that, he was sidetracked by an irate and raccoonish-looking

Mark Albright, who, before Slidell could say "How may I help you?" launched into a disjointed tale about being attacked by Sylvester the Cat who said "What's up, Doc?" instead of "Sufferin' succotash," but who was really Ernie Brown.

This was really quite amusing, and it took great restraint to avoid laughing out loud. After calming Mark, Slidell determined that the attacker wore a mask until Mark lost consciousness, and that Mark never saw his face.

Mark, however, maintained that he knew what Ernie Brown looked like, and that the attacker was Ernie Brown in a Sylvester the Cat mask. Mark refused to budge, saying there was no one else who looked like Ernie Brown in a cat mask but Ernie Brown.

Slidell assured Mark that he would investigate, and sent Mark on his way.

Once again, Slidell found himself believing everything a complainant said, but being unable to prove the case. Ernie Brown was pretty distinctive, but one big guy in a cat mask looked pretty much like another. Besides that, Mark had alleged that some money was missing from his pocket. By his own words, Mark had distanced Ernie as a suspect in Slidell's mind. Ernie's motive was revenge, not money. Slidell figured that Mark had thrown in the bit about money to upgrade a simple assault to a felony strong-armed robbery, since he never mentioned anything about a missing wallet. Yet it was what Mark said, so Slidell had to work it that way.

He was seriously tempted to chalk this one up to street justice, but that wouldn't do. If he turned a blind eye to one such incident, hell, there'd be vigilantes in the street. No, he'd talk to Ernie, and see what he could come up with. But secretly, probably unconsciously, he hoped it would be nothing.

Chapter XIV

Two weeks had passed since Ernie Brown had attacked him in the parking lot of the Surf's Up, and as near as Mark could tell, Slidell Goodbee hadn't done anything.

He could see Ernie sitting down the beach at his concession, smirking probably, in the knowledge that he had gotten away with a vicious assault. Mark apparently overlooked the fact that he had tried to kill Ernie. He had that capability, as some do, of screening out facts that are unpleasant or inconvenient in drawing a desired conclusion from a situation.

As time had passed, Mark had considered many ways of taking righteous retribution, but had reached a temporary standstill. Nothing he had come up with to date would not violate the prime directive, so to speak, as handed down by Farley Tanner: Do nothing to jeopardize the operation.

He realized that bringing attention to Ernie Brown and himself would only provoke more snooping on the part of Slidell Goodbee, and things were already bad enough. It seemed like every time he looked up, he caught the sheriff disappearing along the periphery of his vision. Furthermore, he hadn't noticed any evidence of nighttime skullduggery along the beach or near his beach box.

No. Whatever he decided to do about Ernie Brown would have to be put on hold, or be so convoluted that no one would ever suspect he was involved. And that would take some time to figure out, considering Farley and Billy Boy knew the situation.

Mark concluded that he would direct his energies to something more worthy of his abilities; namely, getting rid of Slidell Goodbee. That would clear him with Tanner and Turman, and then he could deal with Ernest Brown.

Obviously, he reasoned, the gambit with the CIA had not worked. If anything, it had increased Goodbee's monitoring activities. Of course, since the CIA thing was his plan, that hadn't helped his relationship with his boss. Something was called for in the nature of playing a trump card that would scare off the sheriff for good.

In Mark Albright's experience, which was mostly from movies and second-rate detective novels, even a hard case could be gotten to through something he loved. Whereas a direct threat might be taken as a challenge by a strong man, putting something he loved in jeopardy was a different story. Once in an intimate relationship, the male of our species was programmed to protect. It was almost like a fundamental genetic thing. Running from a fight might be cowardice, but withdrawing from conflict to save a loved one was an acceptable, even manly, thing to do.

Aside from his job, the only thing Mark knew of Slidell Goodbee was that he and Daphne Fairhope were an item of long standing.

Mark would have to think about that for a while.

*****

After being connected with many "assistants to the assistant" at Langley, Slidell had finally reached the level of "assistant to" somebody important. The woman was apparently constitutionally opposed to a simple "yes" or "no," and following their conversation, Slidell had the sensation he had been chasing a greased pig. Everything the woman said was from an angle, an answer by implication. But what he finally gleaned was that the CIA had absolutely no interest in Pensacola Beach, probably, at present, to her best understanding, relatively speaking. He had taken that as a "no" and rang off. So if the CIA wasn't involved, what was that call all about? The obvious conclusion was that someone wanted him gone. The far less than obvious question was why.

Once again, Slidell had summoned his war council, this time with a slightly different result. Last time, they had a lot of questions and no answers. This time, they didn't even have any good questions. The only thing they felt fairly certain of was that whatever was cooking, it had to do with that stretch of beach along the front of the Surf's Up. The only thing he knew to do was watch and wait. Maybe something else would happen.

In the cop shows, two detectives would sit in their car eating hamburgers and drinking coffee until something happened. Unfortunately, Slidell didn't have the manpower for even one uniformed officer to sit and watch periodically. So he took a different tact: he made the Surf's Up his place for breakfast, lunch, and dinner, with an occasional look/see thrown in for good measure. His thinking was that if he turned up the pressure, maybe someone would slip up. Although in his heart of hearts he didn't really think that would happen, at least if he was around, perhaps people would stop killing people and throwing them through tenth floor windows.

*****

Using his key to enter Billy Boy Turman's condo after a long day of sitting under an umbrella, Mark caught the beach end of a telephone conversation that he probably wasn't supposed to hear.

"Yes, Farley. I know we're about a month behind, but every time we look up, Slidell Goodbee's here. Who knows what he does at night?" reasoned Turman.

Pause.

"We've been over that. I know we wouldn't be in this position if Albright hadn't come up with his 'brilliant idea,' and weeds wouldn't grow if the sun didn't shine. That's water under the bridge, and it won't do any good to rehash it or do something crazy. We've just got to wait."

Pause.

"I understand the economics, Farley. What is it that you think we should do?"

Pause.

"Well, I don't know either, but let's don't do something strange. Let's just give it some time. Maybe he'll go away, or we'll think of something."

Pause.

"I know. I know. I will." With that, Billy Boy hung up. This clearly wasn't a happy ending.

Deciding that this was not the time to be handy, Mark opted for the condo restroom on the first floor, and left as quietly as he had entered.

Showtime, Mark thought.

*****

Daphne Fairhope's modest dwelling was located in the Gulf Breeze area backing up to Santa Rosa Sound. It wasn't technically Daphne's house, but for all practical purposes it was. Judge and Mrs. Fairhope, Daphne's parents, occupied the family estate in Tallahassee, near the Florida seat of government. As a justice on the Florida Supreme Court, it was necessary for the judge to spend much of his time in the state capital, which left their summer "cottage" vacant.

The cottage was a colonial mansion christened "Fairbreeze," which would have seemed ostentatious except for its size and grounds: twelve thousand square feet on five acres. Two acres of that was shoreline, complete with dock and both sail and motor boats. Fairbreeze was well maintained by a team of gardeners and maids who worked seemingly continuously to make it perhaps one of *the* houses in the Pensacola area.

It was not a good idea to leave the cottage empty, and Daphne certainly had both the time to see that the cottage was well cared for and the inclination to live in the beach area. Ostensibly, Daphne supervised the maintenance of Fairbreeze while pursuing a dilettante version of a career in real estate.

The Fairhope family, at least Daphne's father's branch of it, had been active in local politics in the Pensacola area for a long time, which culminated in Judge Fairhope's appointment to the Supreme Court. Daphne had grown up in the beach community, and had never aspired to anything greater than fun in the sun. Although the Judge and Mrs. were somewhat disappointed as Daphne descended through the college ranks to finally flunk out of the University of West Florida, the last evidence that Daphne was not cut out for any kind of profession coincided with the judge's elevation to the big court in the state capital. It was only fitting that Judge and Mrs. Fairhope live in Tallahassee. This arrangement was especially convenient since Mrs. Fairhope's mother had been widowed several years back, and was having difficulty managing the property.

Slidell had refused to move into Fairbreeze, maintaining he was not going to be thought of as a gigolo. It was therefore necessary for Daphne to spend most nights in Slidell's "little place." Friday, however, was the traditional day on which the princess of the manor inspected the maintenance of Fairbreeze and spent the night. Tradition also dictated that Friday night was the night she called "Daddy and Mother" to report on the state of the cottage.

The comings and goings of Daphne Fairhope were not something that had escaped Mark Albright. Since hatching his scheme to get rid of Slidell Goodbee and simultaneously ingratiate himself with Farley, Mark had shadowed Daphne semi-religiously. Thus he knew that she would be most vulnerable on Friday night alone at Fairbreeze. In addition, of all the places Mark might have paid a little visit, Fairbreeze was the most accessible and least likely to attract any attention to him.

The plot as it played out in Mark's mind was fairly simple. He would "appropriate" a motorboat, and journey across the sound under cover of darkness, where he would tie up on the beachfront at Fairbreeze. Dressed in black, complete with ski mask, he would break into the house, terrorize Daphne, and depart after binding her. Later, by anonymous call, he would advise that if the sheriff didn't lay off the Surf's Up investigation, he'd be back for more than just a chat with Daphne.

Again, this was a serious gamble. If he won, and

his feelings, and it was all Slidell Goodbee's fault. *Why did he always have to be such a dickhead? For Christ's sake, what was this place good for, if you couldn't use it?*

She decided what she needed was a drink, a strong drink. As she watched the fading day, with her second fading drink, her anger turned morose. *Poor little rich girl*, she thought. A self-pitying crying jag was coming on. Fortunately it was a brief one, after which she felt much better and went inside. It was hot and the bugs had descended with the dark.

Well, since I'm solo, I might as well be comfortable, she thought, sloughing her clothes in exchange for a babydoll dressing robe, and going off to see what was available for dinner.

It had been at this time that Mark Albright lurked in the shadows and began moving toward the house. The window was no problem; he easily slipped through to find himself in what appeared to be the laundry room. Gingerly sliding the door open, he encountered the rear end of a heart-stopping Daphne bending at the waist to inspect the contents of the pantry. Before she could say Old Mother Hubbard, she felt an arm slip around her waist, and the sting of something sharp at her throat.

"Don't scream. Do what I say and you might live," croaked a man's voice. To make sure he had her attention, he inflicted a surface neck wound.

As millions of thoughts raced through her head, her worst nightmare was coming true. All she could squeak out was, "Please don't hurt me."

*****

    Earlier, Slidell had given up on paperwork. He was way too irked with the situation to concentrate. He had decided to get it over with, and maybe then he could get some work done.

    In the affairs of the heart, a little time can cool the fire of anger. As Slidell drove, the heat of the phone conversation was replaced with little reminiscences much more in keeping with what was a very good relationship: happy times, passionate times. When he pulled up in the circular drive of Fairbreeze, he was much more in the mood to make up rather than continue the turmoil.

    Curiously, the house was dark; only a slight glow came from within. Of course, he hadn't been inside in a long time, and that was only when the family still stayed there. Then the house was always ablaze with light. Still, he decided he would surprise Daphne, maybe scare the shit out of her as a little payback, so he quietly proceeded through the massive front door.

    Moving in semi-darkness, he sensed something wrong in the atmosphere. Nothing he could describe, just what was left of the primal sixth sense warning. Then he heard the strange little half-sob, "Please don't hurt me," and, with cop's reflexes, knew this was no game.

    Pulling his .44 magnum from its clipped holster in the small of his back, he dropped to a two-handed shooting stance as he rounded the corner to the kitchen. Sizing up the situation instantly, he made the almost deafening command, "Freeze, motherfucker. Drop the knife."

Mark indeed froze. *How could this be happening?* he thought. *This wasn't supposed to be the way it went.* Mark didn't drop the knife. Maybe he was caught, but he wasn't captured. He turned and stared into the cold dead eyes of Slidell Goodbee for what seemed like several minutes.

"You drop the gun, asshole, or I'll slit her from ear to ear," challenged Mark.

The "Mexican standoff." Mark figured, as he'd figured all along, that Slidell wouldn't risk the woman. He'd seen this a dozen times on TV. Once Slidell had dropped the gun, well… in for a penny, in for a pound.

Slidell, who had his gun aimed at Mark's head, knew that if he dropped the gun, he'd be the second victim. So he did what anyone with any sense, even someone who wasn't a highly practiced marksman, would have done. He pulled the trigger. Mark and most of Mark's head hit the refrigerator before he could think the word "cut."

Like they say, too much TV can be bad for you.

Chapter XV

Farley Tanner sat thinking, more like fuming, since that was his mood coupled with the smoke from a fat black cigar which he held tightly clenched in his teeth. He was seated on his bathroom throne reading the *News Journal's* account of the death of Mark Albright for the third or fourth time. Actually, "reading" would not be technically correct, as his eyes were only loosely focused on the print with no real comprehension of the content.

What could that Albright kid have been thinking, Tanner wondered, *breaking into Daphne Fairhope's house?* The whole thing made no sense to him as any part of a rational plan. He could only chalk it off to the work of a perverse, demented personality. How had he so badly misjudged the boy? Everybody has a little larceny in their soul; Mark, he had figured, more than most. But a little, even a lot, of healthy larceny was a bit different than burglary of a habitation with intent to commit sexual assault and who knows what else. And to Daphne, of all people; he'd have to patch that up.

Now, because of Farley's misjudgment, Slidell Goodbee was even more of a problem, and they had no beach boy to watch after the operation during the daytime.

Maybe, somehow, that pervert Billy Boy Turman had perverted Albright, Farley thought. He knew he should never have gotten involved with Turman in the first place, but several things made Turman a good candidate for an accomplice. Billy Boy had the legal knowledge, the location, and he had known Tanner in his other life. If he hadn't cut him in, no telling what he might have done.

Anyway, what was done was done. Now the problem was how to get the treasure out, given the new and more difficult circumstances. Anybody with any damn sense, he calculated, would shut down and try again some other time. But there were problems with the smart course of action. There were now eight people that he knew of, other than himself, who knew the deal. Just because he called it off didn't mean one or more of the other eight might not try to slip in and make off with the goods. After all, they were all thieves. Also, although they had located the treasure, there was no guarantee that the gulf wouldn't reclaim her bounty. A hurricane or a shift in the ocean current might cover what they had found with millions of tons of sand or simply relocate it. And, of course, there was the chance that someone else would make the same discovery.

All that, plus the fact that Farley was sick to death of the gospel game. If he had to listen to "Bringing in the Sheaves" one more time, he feared he would throw up. He was disgusted in the depths of his little black soul with people who would believe anything if he told them the Bible said so.

"Bringing in the Sheaves?" Shit. "Bringing in the Suckers" was more like it. *If there was a God, surely he was mightily amused with the foolishness of his creations.*

There had to be a better solution, but if there was, he couldn't think of it. Slidell Goodbee was the problem, and the problem would just have to be eliminated. But he'd give it some more time. Maybe that pervert Turman would have some ideas, but he doubted it. Turman was a chickenshit fag who never wanted to do anything dangerous. Turman would probably rather let the gold be carried away by beach hippies than get his hands dirty.

*****

One good thing about the mayhem at Fairbreeze was that Daphne had no inclination to ever spend the night there again. At least that was the way Slidell saw it. Daphne now spent all her nights at Slidell's condominium, and was now peacefully sleeping beside him.

Slidell, on the other hand, was not peacefully sleeping; far from it. Something terrible was going on here, and he still had no idea what. He sure wished, in retrospect, that he had not been such a good shot. Less than a nanosecond after he had squeezed the trigger, Mark Albright had become the late Mark Albright, and sure couldn't tell him what he was doing at Fairbreeze, or how his being there was connected with the Surf's Up, if it was. Slidell couldn't prove the two were connected, but he just knew they were, somehow.

Slidell had gone through all the right moves in a homicide investigation/police shooting. He had even suspended himself, pending the results of the investigation and grand jury action, if any. He had been exonerated, but nothing worthwhile had turned up on the late Mark Albright. The official conclusion concerning the incident was that the Albright boy was a random rapist who selected the wrong victim and probably got just what he deserved. Case closed.

Although that was the official conclusion, it was wrong in Slidell's opinion. Mark Edward Albright had been an average student at Grimsley High School in Greensboro, North Carolina. His only extracurricular activity centered around his parents' ministry. Everyone interviewed remembered him as a good boy who never got into any trouble. Of course, he had no criminal record there. He left Greensboro after high school graduation, never to be seen in the area again. Even his parents had had no contact with their son.

Then, three years later, the new Albright with a lengthy rapsheet surfaced in Pensacola Beach working as a beach vendor. After a few months of nothing out of the ordinary, he apparently tried to kill another beach vendor, and shortly thereafter, broke into a mansion in the nicest part of town and tried to rape a prominent citizen.

The manager of the Surf's Up had reported that Albright had shown up on the heels of the disappearance of the former beach attendant, giving Farley Tanner as a reference. William Turman had appeared to take Albright under his wing, and the two had established an ostensibly close relationship.

What did that all mean? wondered Slidell. He needed to have a talk with Tanner and Turman. Maybe that would shed some light on the mystery, but he doubted it. Things just weren't falling neatly into place.

*****

Ernie Brown was perched on a stool at the Islander Bar, pontificating to a couple of local, semi-employed fishermen-carpenters-whatever-they-could-get.

"I knew there was something wrong with Albright the first time I saw the son of a bitch. He just didn't fit – too clean cut. Then that deal with the funny tool, and then he tries to run me down. But to tell you the truth, I didn't have him pegged as a rapist," allowed Ernie.

"Well," responded old Drew, a slight, wiry type, "one thing I do know is this ol' boy ain't gonna be fuckin' around with Sheriff Goodbee. He flat put him down. Heard it was a single shot right between the runnin' lights. Bingo!" he said, making a gun with his hand and blowing imaginary smoke from the barrel.

"On the other hand," chipped in the bartender, "Daphne Fairhope might tempt a man." The conversants turned to eye the bartender incredulously. "I mean, might tempt a man to risk tanglin' with Goodbee for a date with her, or somethin'."

"Um hmm," taunted Caesar the Greek. They all shared a knowing look at the bartender's expense.

"Hey, come on, dudes. I ain't no rapist. But I heard ol' Honest Ernest here moved pretty quick for Albright's part of the beach," the bartender said, trying hard to change the subject.

"Hey, it's a free country. Somebody's gotta take up the slack," responded Ernie.

As a point of fact, shortly after the beach grapevine spread the news of Mark Albright's demise, Ernie Brown was at the Surf's Up talking to the manager about replacing Albright as the beach vendor. Having no reason not to give the concession to Ernie and no one else around to supply his tenants, he had given Ernie the job.

It hadn't gone as smoothly as Ernie had figured, though.

The first problem was the beach box was locked, and he had to break in to get the chairs and umbrellas, which turned out not to be there. There was just a bunch of machinery that no one seemed to know anything about, and no beach rigs anywhere.

Investigating further, it seemed that Mark Albright had kept all of his equipment in his van, which was unfortunately in the possession of the sheriff's department. Since the sheriff wasn't about to release something that might be evidence in a murder investigation, it had been a mad scramble to put together enough rigs to service the Surf's Up.

Now Ernie was even deeper in debt, and wondering just how smart he had been, moving so quickly on Albright's old area.

After an hour or so of "honkin' the gristle," an expression Ernie had heard some Yankee use for "chewin' the fat," he'd had enough beer and enough gristle.

"You ol' beach buzzards can hang around drinkin' half the night, but us captains of industry got to get up in the morning," he said by way of farewell as he settled up his tab. His old bike was still a crumpled mass, so he was hoofin' it, hoping no one else wanted to run him down, and wondering about his new beach box.

Keeping a wary eye on car lights while he thought, Ernie pictured the inside of his new beach box again. Never having much of a mechanical aptitude, the use of the contraption he had discovered was not immediately apparent. However, even a psychology major could deduce that the great long hoses were for blowing or sucking, and since there wasn't anything around for blowing, he decided that what he had was a giant vacuum cleaner, and the curious tool he and Mark

Albright had fought over had to be some sort of handle for the hose.

He supposed the vacuum could be for picking up trash, but that was a lot of machine for what little trash accumulated on the beaches around here. Maybe for seaweed, he wondered. Sometimes the tide brought a lot of the stuff in, and nobody, especially the tourists, liked having it lying around. On the other hand, the Santa Rosa Island Authority had a big raking machine to pick up the seaweed. Maybe this was just extra protection.

Ernie was thinking hard now, and didn't notice the big white convertible parked just down the street from his house.

*****

Billy Boy and Farley sat waiting in Ernie's darkened house.

It had been difficult convincing Farley not to give Ernie the Scudder VanAlstine treatment, but Billy Boy was really sick of all these people getting killed. He had reasoned with Farley, as well as a person could reason with Farley Tanner, to at least feel Ernie out on working with the operation. If he seemed hesitant, or balked outright, then more drastic measures might be in order. Billy Boy didn't like that part, or the fact that Farley had a nine millimeter tucked in his coat, but he had to give up something or Farley would never have agreed. Besides, he had urged, Ernie had started his career on the island as a petty thief, so he certainly wasn't above walking on the other side of the law. Not to mention, they didn't have another candidate for the job, and someone had to do it and soon, or they'd never get the treasure out.

This last argument seemed to weigh heaviest on Farley. Farley wanted the gold, now. Also Billy Boy figured that even Farley recognized that they couldn't just keep killing people every time something went wrong.

So here they sat. Farley had been pacing until he had tripped over an ottoman or something. Billy Boy sat, and was beginning to sweat, more from nerves than from heat. Billy Boy hated that. Sweating was not neat and tidy, and Billy Boy despised anything not neat and tidy.

*****

The minute Ernie stepped into his house, he knew something was not right without having to turn on the light. Of course, when he did turn on the light, he could see things were not as he'd left them. He just barely knew Turman and Tanner, and he certainly wouldn't have left them in his living room.

"Hey! What the fuck you guys doing in here?" he bellowed, a combination of anger and fear.

"Easy now, Ernie," Billy Boy soothed. "This is the only way we could talk to you in private without anyone knowing."

"Talk to me about what? What don't you want anyone to know?" queried Ernie, incredulous, as his fear gave way to plain old pissed off.

"Now just hear us out. I think you'll like what we have

to say, and understand why we had to go this route," explained Billy Boy, again the peacemaker.

Farley surreptitiously stroked his gun. "We heard you took over the beach concession at the Surf's Up, and we've got a business deal for you, if you're the right person." This time Tanner did the talking.

Ernie took a deep breath, brought himself under control, and stepped back. *Who knows what these guys want?* thought Ernie. *But they're both rich and powerful. Wouldn't hurt to hear them out; besides, I could use the money.* Ernie had also noticed the unsightly bulge in Farley Tanner's coat, and just made a wild guess that it wasn't a Bible. So he sat and spread his hands as if to say *OK, let's hear it.*

Alternately explaining parts of the operation, Tanner and Turman got the story out, emphasizing the huge profits that could be made if the government didn't find out.

As they seemed to conclude, Ernie's most pressing thought was, *What if I say no?* However, he recalled the absence of the last two beach concessionaires at the Surf's Up, and that bulge in Tanner's coat. So he asked the penultimate question, "What's in it for me?"

Turman and Tanner exchanged a look, and Tanner continued. "We figure that you'll get all the profits from the beach concession." He raised his hands, as if to say *Just wait, that's not all*, when Ernie rolled his eyes. "Plus two percent of the total take. That two percent could be as much as a million dollars. We don't know for sure. Right now two percent is about twenty thousand dollars, and we haven't even scratched the surface. What with people getting killed and the laws all over the place, our mining time has been almost nothing."

Tanner and Turman both paused, waiting expectantly.

"Do you need an answer right now?" asked Ernie. His first impulse had been to throw them out, but the prospect of money for nothing piqued his greed. Like the cartoon said: the upside was fabulous wealth; the downside was eight hundred hours of community service. Then, of course, there was that bulge in Tanner's coat.

"Yes, Ernie, we need to know right now," answered Tanner with the levity of a mortician.

Ernie feigned deep thought, then said, "OK, I'm in. What do I do?"

Ernie's response caused Billy Boy to audibly release his breath and Farley's brow to furrow. Clearly, Farley Tanner wasn't immediately buying Ernie's decision, and who knew what Billy Boy was really thinking, other than feeling relief for the time being. Notwithstanding any reservations they may have had, they explained what was required over and above the beach concession: mostly just keep an eye out, and be on call if needed.

With their business concluded, they shook hands before leaving, as Tanner continued to give Ernie a piercing stare, apparently believing that, if he looked hard enough, he could spot betrayal.

Driving back to America, Farley squirmed and dodged

in an attempt to hide his presence from anyone who might be interested. Billy Boy relaxed a little, hoping his stomach wouldn't give him trouble that night. They both agreed that this was a gamble, but a necessary one. Ernie Brown would bear watching. He'd be on terminal probation.

Ernie had turned the light off again, and sat in the dark drinking his last beer while he considered his position. This was the kind of deal where he was in or out, right now. He couldn't just go along for a while. That would be like trying to be just a little pregnant. He was either going to be a snitch or a real criminal, and he had to decide before he showed up on the beach the next day. Playing along for even a little while would mean he was immediately an accomplice to only-God-knows-what; certainly larceny, maybe murder.

Chapter XVI

In difficult circumstances, Ernie tended to fall back on previous learning: What would Kwai Chang Caine have done in this situation? Although it sounded stupid – basing a decision on what a fictitious TV character might have done – it had always worked before. Of course, once the decision was made, he never really knew how another course of action might have resulted, but he seemed to still be alive and fairly healthy. So, what the hell, the Kwai Chang Decision Paradigm was as good as any. And that's why he was creeping around the residence of Slidell Goodbee in the dark at four o'clock in the morning.

Ernie had reasoned that going to see the sheriff in broad daylight would probably be the "go" signal for Tanner and Turman to end Ernie's brief existence. Since tomorrow was decision time, he had to get to Goodbee before anyone was up and about. That meant a house call. When he made the big decision, he hadn't put much thought into the details of approaching a man who had the license for, and lacked any qualms about, shooting alleged bad guys. But now, in the dark, outside the sheriff's residence, he recalled that it hadn't been too long since this same man had taken out another beach dude right over the left shoulder of his lady love.

Deciding that throwing pebbles at Slidell's window was like putting a target on his forehead, Ernie had elected to try the direct approach, and hoped no one saw him ringing the sheriff's doorbell.

In fairly short order, the porch light came on, followed by a gruff "Who's there?"

"Ernie Brown," squeaked Ernie.

"Who? Goddammit, speak up," directed the sheriff in his best cop voice.

"Ernie Brown," said Ernie, shoring up his courage.

"Who?... What the hell are you doing here at this hour? What do you want?" demanded the sheriff.

This is not a good question, Ernie thought. Screaming he was here to snitch off Turman and Tanner in the quiet predawn morning just wouldn't work out. Ernie elected to disguise his voice.

"I need to speak to you right now, Sheriff. It's a matter of life and death," squealed Ernie, as he slipped into falsetto. Nobody was going to recognize that voice.

On the other hand, Slidell became immediately convinced that he was dealing with a drugged-out crazy person.

"Click click" went the locks.

"Kabam" went the door.

And one of the largest gun barrels Ernie had ever seen was pointed right between his eyes. Ernie had an unfortunate accident.

"Down on the ground, asshole!" screamed Slidell Goodbee.

Ernie complied immediately, only remembering his mission and the jeopardy he was in after he had assumed a prone position. "Sheriff. Sheriff. I'm not crazy," Ernie whispered, simultaneously thinking that he was going to have a really hard time selling that. "I've got to see you without anyone seeing me." *Shit*, Ernie thought. "I mean no one can know I'm talking to you. I don't mean I want to be invisible. If you'll just let me in, I can talk regular."

Slidell thought this over, realizing things were pretty crazy around the beach anyway, and maybe Ernie knew something. "OK. But I want you to stay down, and if you do anything but crawl in there and stop..." Ernie understood.

Slowly Ernie crawled, more like slithered, into the front room of the sheriff's condo. As soon as Slidell could shut the door, he cuffed Ernie's hands behind his back, and searched him. Considering Ernie's accident, this was not something Slidell enjoyed, but he was reassured when he found no weapon.

"Would you like to tell me something before we adjourn to my place of business?" mocked Slidell.

With as much dignity as a person can manage handcuffed on his belly, reeking of urine, Ernie told the story. Slidell listened, and to his amazement, he believed Honest Ernest Brown for the second time in less than a year.

As the sky began to turn a vivid pink, Ernie Brown slipped out of Slidell Goodbee's home. This time he was standing up.

*****

Beach days passed, one pretty much like another, as Ernie "led three lives" – beach vendor, criminal, and snitch. As a practical matter, the only noticeable difference was that Ernie's general level of anxiety increased. Slidell Goodbee went through the motions of rousting Ernie once a week or so, as a guise for getting any useful information Ernie might have learned. There was nothing new about that. Ernie had only limited contact with "the gang" through Billy Boy Turman, who occasionally rented an umbrella rig and asked if things were OK. Things were OK. He never noticed anything, except that the sand around his beach box was unusually ruffled some mornings. To the outside world, Ernie was just the beach guy, going about his business. And, in fact, that's what he was doing, but inwardly he had the constant feeling that something very bad was about to happen.

Then one hazy hot day, Billy Boy Turman approached him, skipping the customary rental ruse, and told him to come up to his condo that evening. This was not a request.

Cutting straight to the chase, Turman had instructed

Ernie that he would be needed that night, no "ifs," "buts," or "if you can make its." Turman had simply said, "Be on the beach at two-thirty tonight, and wear a wet suit. It's time for you to start earning your money." End of story.

Luckily, Ernie had a wet suit, but that was the least of his worries. *What,* he wondered, as he sat in his darkened house, *will I be required to do?* A wet suit usually meant getting wet, but beyond that he didn't know. Maybe he would be using the big hose, or maybe Turman and Tanner had discovered he was a snitch for Sheriff Goodbee. He really needed to get in touch with the sheriff. But how could he do that without guaranteeing the gang would know he was a snitch? He didn't have a weapon, and if he did, he couldn't very well secret it away in his wet suit. These thoughts reverberated through his head as he waited for the time of departure.

Kwai Chang, uncharacteristically, had nothing to say.

Thinking that driving his new beach van, supplied by Turman, would not be very clandestine, he got in the spirit of things and cut across the island, near the Emerald Isle condos, and hiked down the beach. As he scuttled toward the Surf's Up, mentally picturing himself as Kwai Chang Caine in a wet suit, he seemed to have blocked out the very real possibility that he might be about to take a long swim at the behest of Turman and Tanner. He was now the Shaolin monk who could walk through walls, invisible against the black of a moonless gulf.

Lost in his reverie, Ernie had skulked almost past the Surf's Up, when he was brought up short by an angry voice he did not recognize.

"Hey, beach dude! We're over here."

Squinting, Ernie could make out the five black-clad figures seated beside his beach box.

"Where the hell were you going?" ask one of the shadowy figures, clearly wearing a wet suit not unlike Ernie's.

"Reconnoitering the area?" Ernie advanced weakly.

One guy to his left rolled his eyes and said, "Oh, great."

"OK. Look," said the figure who had hailed him, "here's the deal. One of our regular guys is out. You're his replacement. All you gotta do is let the hose out and pull it in when we say, and make sure it don't get tangled. Can you do that?"

Ernie said "Sure" enthusiastically, but he was inwardly disappointed. Somewhere in his mind's eye he had envisioned crawling around with a knife between his teeth taking out sentries.

Blinking his flashlight once in the direction of the roof of the Surf's Up, the guy who seemed to be in charge said, "Let's do it then," and the action began.

Two of the team immediately scurried off in opposite directions on the beach. One guy moved to the water, and the head guy helped Ernie get the hose unraveled and the vacuum turned on. Then he went to the water as well. Ernie stood by the beach box, trying to look like a commando, and occasionally let out more hose or wound it in, as directed by the two in the surf.

Two hours passed in this fashion. Ernie decided the

commando/criminal routine wasn't what it's cracked up to be in the movies. In fact, this was boring as hell. Every so often, something would rattle through the hose. Ernie imagined this to be a golden scepter or bejeweled crown stolen from the aboriginal inhabitants of Pensacola Bay. Otherwise, this was about as much fun as filing student information cards at the Admin Building at North Texas.

Finally, the head guy signaled Ernie to take the hose in, after which, through a series of flashlight blinks, the lookouts joined them at the beach box.

"You did fine, pal," the head guy said to Ernie. "Turman'll let you know if we need you again."

With that, the gang vanished like cockroaches in a kitchen when the light comes on, leaving Ernie standing in the dark next to his box.

*****

"So, I guess you were right, Turman," concluded Tanner reluctantly, referring to Ernie's performance to date. "He comes through when we need him and, in the meantime, keeps his mouth shut and stays outta trouble."

Billy Boy Turman smiled inwardly. He loved it when he was right and Farley Tanner was wrong. But he didn't love it when he had to meet with Tanner, for two reasons. The first was his own natural inclination to avoid difficulties, and any time he had to meet with Tanner, it was not a pleasurable thing. The second was that they couldn't just call each other or meet for lunch at McGuire's. It was always this big secret deal.

This time he had to jog eight miles down Fort Pickens Road to the fort, then pretend he was wandering around the ramparts while Farley walked beside him, but six feet lower and on the side of the wall hidden from view. He felt stupid, and it was hot, and when the whole stupid thing was over, he'd have to jog eight miles back to the Surf's Up.

"The boys tell me pickins is slim," said Tanner, looking up at Billy Boy Turman's disgustingly skimpy jogging shorts. "Maybe the motherlode's run out. If that's the case, we got a problem."

Tanner paused pregnantly.

For effect, Billy Boy thought, but he bit anyway. "What's our problem?" Billy Boy asked, playing the straight man.

"By my count, the take to date is about three million, and there's eight people that we have to divide by. That's roughly four hundred thou per, less whatever we give the beach dude. After expenses, the take home doesn't really make my eyes sparkle."

Billy Boy Turman's stomach began to churn. Although the thought hadn't crystallized, something primordial recognized a bad moon rising. Consciously shutting his mind, he replied, "So what're you saying?" He didn't look down because he didn't want to see the look on Farley's face.

"If we didn't have to divide by so many people, maybe only by two, we'd make a tidy sum. Enough for me to maybe retire, for a while at least." Tanner paused again. "You get the picture, Billy Boy?"

Billy Boy got the picture OK. "Farley, if I understand correctly, you're proposing that we kill seven people." He knew without looking that Tanner was smiling that wicked smile of his. He also knew this was the kind of offer he couldn't turn down. He could be in, or he could be dead. What he didn't know was why he'd been given the choice in the first place. He'd find out soon.

"I believe you get the picture. After we eliminate the division problem, we shut down and bide our time. You keep an eye on the area, and maybe later, if it looks promising, we start up again. Whadaya think?" Farley waited again.

Billy Boy was now looking forward to the jog home; it would give him time to think, and maybe stop his stomach from churning. But for now, he replied, "You know I don't like all this killing. I never bargained for this." Again his options intervened, and he continued, "On the other hand, a million and a half has a much better sound than two or three hundred thousand. Would you be taking care of the... eh... problem?"

"Now you're talking. Down deep, I always knew that limp-wristed fag thing was just an act. I knew you were a greedy soulless bastard, just like me. Hell, you're a lawyer." Farley laughed. "Yeah, to answer your question, I'll handle the details. You just be handy if something unusual comes up. And hold down the fort, so it'll still be available if it becomes profitable again further on down the road. We don't want the damn county commissioners deciding to tear down the Surf's Up to build a park, or selling out to some high-rise developer."

"One thing, Farley." Billy Boy's mind was working overtime. "The wet team won't be missed, but if the beach guy disappears, someone will likely get curious. You know, that would be the third one."

"Hmmm. Maybe so. I'll think about it," answered Tanner, sounding unhappy that Billy Boy had thought of something he hadn't, or perhaps disappointed that he couldn't take out all of them.

There followed a long silence, and when Billy Boy did look down, Farley was gone. Just before he threw up, Billy Boy was thinking that, despite all, he had to admire Farley's flair for the dramatic.

*****

Slidell sat in his darkened office, the day staff at the office long since gone home. From the streaks of pink and green now cloaking the gulf, he concluded it must have been a spectacular sunset. He hadn't noticed. His thoughts had been focused on the conversation he had had with Ernie Brown fifteen hours before, in which Ernie had explained the prior night's skullduggery.

It seemed that what he had here was a pretty straightforward case of treasure hunters trying to evade government control.

Hell, it probably isn't even in my jurisdiction, he thought. But something had kept him from picking up the phone, and turning it over to the feds. Perhaps it was the feeling that all the stuff that had gone on around the Surf's Up was somehow connected to the treasure hunting. Those other things (murder, arson, attempted rape, burglary) were definitely his business.

The problem was how to tie it up. Although he now knew what was going on, he still didn't have any solid proof that any of the treasure hunters were involved. It seemed reasonable that the lieutenant had stumbled onto the operation and been killed to avoid further detection. It was likely that the body ended up where it did while it was being hauled up to Billy Boy Turman's condo for disposal. The beach box explosion could have been because it was simply too close to the action. But who knew what happened to Scudder VanAlstine, or why? And Mark Albright didn't fit at all. And assuming that there was a rational connection, so what? Who would he charge? Tanner, Turman, and six nameless guys in wet suits? And why? Because he had a gut feeling?

Nope. He needed something else to make it work, and he didn't want to give it to the feds until he had that something. What did they care about his little state crimes? They'd charge all six guys, let three guys off for testifying against the other three, and they'd all get probation and a stern rebuke. In the process, they'd screw up any possibility of solving his cases, and just for good measure, they'd create some kind of double jeopardy problems in the off-chance he ever did bring the bad guys to trial.

What he needed to do was take care of his own business first. Screw the feds. He'd play the fed game, but he'd play first and with his own witness, a person up to his elbows in the dirty deeds, who might be willing to turn state's evidence for the proper consideration. The face that immediately materialized was Billy Boy Turman. However, he still needed something solid on Turman for a little leverage. Perhaps Ernie Brown would be enough.

Chapter XVII

Once again Billy Boy Turman was doing something strange at the insistence of Farley Tanner: paddling a kayak due south from the Surf's Up, and wondering just how this was going to get him in touch with Farley Tanner. He supposed that Tanner would be out here in some kind of a boat; but at the moment, he didn't see any sort of craft and his arms were beginning to tire. Besides that, the sun beat down mercilessly, and he was now considering that this might be some kind of gay-bashing joke that Tanner would find amusing.

"Kathump."

Something hit his kayak, and fear immediately ran up his back like a jolt of electricity. *Shark!* was his first thought. *I'll be eaten alive, and no one will ever know what happened to me.*

"Kathunk."

Billy Boy's eyes began to well up with tears. There were so many things he hadn't done. *Why now, Lord?*

Then a terrible gurgling sound. It almost sounded like the ferocious leviathan was laughing before his meal

The sound again.

"Hey, that was laughing," Billy Boy said out loud, and as he looked down and to his left, there was Farley Tanner in full scuba gear.

For the next few minutes, Farley said nothing intelligible. In fact, he was laughing so hard, Billy Boy thought he might drown. He hoped he would drown. Finally, under control, Farley said, "Neat deal, huh?"

"You're a bitch. A cold blooded bitch," spluttered Billy Boy.

This brought on another spasm of laughter. "Easy now, Billy. I didn't really mean to scare you. It's just a good way to avoid anyone nosing into our affairs. Keep the kayak between me and the shore."

As Billy Boy calmed, Farley continued. "I was thinking, and decided you were right. We can't take out the beach boy. That's the good news." With that he broke into another bout of giggling. "No. No. I'm sorry. It's just that you looked like somebody was gonna eat you when I came up. Now the bad news is," Farley's expression sobered as he leveled his voice, "I'm gonna need your help. I want you to buy a little beach dinghy. Buy a good one; one that'll hold seven men. You see, it has to look like a toy, but be able to hold you and the wet team. Get 'em together around three next Wednesday, just like we was gonna do the usual, but tell 'em this time it's for a meet. Then you guys row out just like you did today. I'll be here in a boat.

"In fact, get the dinghy tomorrow. Get Ernie to blow it up for you. Go out and paddle around. Hell, take a friend or two. Show everybody who's interested that it's your new toy. Then store it at the beach box. Get Ernie to tie it down with something. Then nobody's gonna be suspicious when you leave it on the beach Wednesday, and it'll be ready to go when you and the wet team meet up. Once you get to the boat, I'll handle the rest."

Billy Boy had thought to protest, but that was probably futile. He didn't want to be part of whatever Tanner was planning for the wet team. Now he paddled back to shore wishing it had been a shark. At least his stomach wouldn't hurt so bad now.

*****

Billy Boy had done as he'd been told. If it hadn't been that he knew something awful was going to happen, it could have been a fun day frolicking with three of his friends from the club. As it was, he was miserable. Even the mai tais hadn't cheered him up, and everybody went home early. *What a soirée disaster*, he thought.

Now he was rowing out into an inky Gulf of Mexico with the wet team. If Farley had placed a special order with

God, it couldn't have been better. The night was moonless and overcast. Only the tiny lights of distant freighters slowly making their way to Pensacola Pass were visible. Gradually what had at first appeared to be a dark lump began to take on the proportions of an old cabin cruiser. Per arrangement, one flash from the dinghy brought a return flash from the boat. It wasn't possible in this light to tell the color of the craft, but it clearly wasn't white; maybe some kind of stained wood. In any case, it was old and big.

As they tied up, boarded the boat, and took seats here and there, Tanner offered everyone a beer, except Billy Boy. He didn't like beer, but he was surprised to find that his glass contained water. After exchanging greetings, Tanner proposed a toast to the operation. This was a bit unusual, but considering the circumstances of the meeting, not all that unusual.

Tanner then began to brief the group, as was his custom in prior gatherings. "Boys, we've been pretty successful, but it looks now like the mine is about tapped out," he began, and then enumerated the take so far, item by item, assigning a value to each.

Billy Boy soon became bored, but noticed that the others were even more so. In fact, fifteen minutes into the briefing, he noticed that everybody but he and Farley had apparently dozed off. When he looked at Farley, Farley had stopped talking and was moving from man to man, gently shaking each. When none of the wet team could be stirred, Farley looked at Billy Boy.

Responding to Billy Boy's look of terror and disgust,

Southern Lights

Farley assured him, "Don't look so scared. You don't have to slit their throats or anything, and they're not dead. They're just passed out. And they're gonna be passed out for a long time. There was enough Valium in those beers to give everybody in Pensacola a good night's sleep. All you gotta do is drag 'em down below. Then help me with the axes."

Again Billy Boy's expression gave away his revulsion.

"No," Farley said. "We're not gonna chop 'em up. We're gonna chop a good hole in the bottom of this piece of shit so it'll sink to the bottom, then haul ass back to the Surf's Up. Can you handle that?"

With Turman's nod, they set to their task: Farley to see his plan to its conclusion; Billy Boy so he wouldn't end up on this boat's last voyage. In less than a half-hour, Turman and Tanner were sitting in their dinghy watching the cabin cruiser's bow slide below the waves. Tanner nodded and smiled at his handiwork. Turman looked ill.

*****

Slidell almost never talked shop with Daphne. Cop work was about one-third boring, one-third exciting, and one-third so disgusting that normal civilians didn't want to hear about it. But he knew, by the way she reacted to him, that he must give off some kind of special vibes when things at work got difficult. Of course, maybe he just got harder to live with. Whatever. When Daphne took a more passive, accommodating approach to their relationship, Slidell knew he must be taking work stress home with him. This was one of those times.

Apparently deciding that Slidell was more stressed than usual, Daphne had asked him what was wrong.

For a moment, Slidell had considered running through the problem and his solution with Daphne, but decided otherwise. Why burden her with this mess? Although she was a smart woman, she wasn't conversant with the intricacies of criminal law, and he didn't have time to educate her enough to help.

"Oh, it's nothing," he mumbled. "Just wrapping up something at the beach."

For days Slidell had considered the alternate ways he might put a stop to this mini-crime spree. Finally, he had decided that his best shot was to confront Turman with what he did know, imply he knew much more, and threaten him with the federal rap, if he didn't 'fess up. For this, he needed Ernie Brown, which was easy enough.

He cornered Ernie one night as he came out of the Islander. Slipping into Ernie's new van, they drove east down Via de Luna toward Navarre Beach. No one was ever out there much after dark, so there was little chance of being seen together.

The plan was simple. Slidell would confront Turman at his condo the next day. Ernie's part was just to accompany the sheriff, and try to look like he was willing to finger Turman and Tanner, but not happy about it. He was not required to say anything. He was only the tangible evidence that Slidell could back up his threats, if Turman decided to tough it out.

Just in case Ernie had any misgivings about going public as a snitch, Slidell alluded to his lack of control over the feds, should they decide that Ernie was not a good guy. That is, if someone neglected to tell them that Ernie was undercover for the sheriff. Ernie seemed quite enthusiastic about cooperating.

*****

Ernie was the front man, knocking on Billy Boy's door while Slidell stood to one side. When the sheriff followed Ernie through the door, Turman should have been shocked, but he wasn't. His look was one of resignation, or at least that's how Slidell took it.

After assuring himself they were alone, Slidell began. "I know what you've got going here, and you're looking at some serious time. Maybe even Ol' Sparky, unless you cooperate. But the way I figure it, Tanner is the man in charge, and he's the one I want to take the hardest fall. If you cooperate, I think we can work a deal that will get you out of prison before you're too old to have a life. Your choice," instructed Slidell, as he moved for his handcuffs.

Turman stiffened, taking on the look of a lawyer who was about to make some constitutional demand, but then he relaxed – collapsed was more like it – and sat down on the sofa. Slidell had no way of knowing about the episode on the boat the night before, or the guilt it had instilled in Turman, along with the belief that he would surely be immediately punished for his role. Turman knew this was coming, and, if the truth were known, he wanted it.

"I'll tell you whatever you want to know, Sheriff," moaned Turman, and he did, right into Slidell's tape recorder after he was Mirandized.

As it turned out, Slidell had most of it figured out. Apparently, no one knew for sure why Albright had decided to break into Daphne's home. But the part that strained even the sheriff's ability to maintain a neutral demeanor was the prior night's boat ride.

Ernie was not so professional. "Holy shit! All of 'em?" he exclaimed, before the sheriff could silence him with a look.

Slidell had planned to keep Turman hidden until the grand jury could meet, but then he hadn't planned on having six more murders to deal with. He felt sure that the sheriff's department's divers could easily recover the bodies, and coupled with the confession, that spelled a lay-down case against Tanner and Turman. Looked like he wasn't kidding about Ol' Sparky, at least for someone.

"Billy Boy," Slidell began, using his nickname unconsciously because he almost felt sorry for him. Turman's narrative had made it seem that he had been victimized by Tanner as well. But, of course, nobody had really twisted his arm, and he could have gotten out before the first murder. "Looks like I'm gonna have to book you, but I'll do what I can for you when it comes to getting a plea deal."

With that, he cuffed Turman, and immediately called his chief deputy for an emergency meeting at his office. This would have to be kept under wraps until he arrested Tanner. Otherwise, he figured Tanner would run. In a deal like this, Tanner had nothing to lose, and Slidell didn't want a firefight. Any number of bad things could happen if Tanner got word before the sheriff showed up on his doorstep.

Chapter XVIII

Because nothing moves fast enough when you want it to, it had taken Slidell three hours to get organized and in position at the Gospel House Church of God. The Gospel House was an old one-story structure that looked to have had three bedrooms at one time, but now functioned as a meeting place and office for Farley Tanner's ministry. The house was located in old Pensacola on residential Gadsden Street, but looked like it would have been more appropriate on several hundred acres of farm land.

One of the jobs of Farley's young proselytes was upkeep of the Gospel House, so the house itself and the grounds were immaculate, making it stand out in a neighborhood that looked as tired as its residents probably were. The giant cross on the roof, above the words GOSPEL HOUSE

CHURCH OF GOD, also tended to draw attention.

But it wasn't any of these things that served to highlight the Gospel House Church of God on this day. It was the four Escambia County Sheriff's Department cars, the van saying SWAT TEAM, and the dozen uniformed men armed to the teeth lurking around every conceivable means of exit from the premises.

Slidell, while dispatching his cadre of officers, noted that Tanner's car was in the garage in the back of the house, and there was a light on somewhere in a back room. One of the things he liked least about being the head man was that he had to take the lead in situations like this. He could have delegated this duty to his chief deputy, but, in his opinion, if you wanted your men to do something, you had to show them that you were willing to do it too. This was especially so with things that might result in their death.

Swallowing his fear, he moved cautiously toward the front door. He sensed no movement from the interior as he approached the door. Demonstrating the technique he had taught his men, he knocked three times loudly, and moved to the side – just in case someone inside decided to take a gratuitous shot through the door. No answer forthcoming, again he knocked loudly and announced, "Police, open up!" Again there was silence.

Of course, it was possible that Tanner wasn't there. But Turman had said he would be. Plus, there was his car in the garage and the light on in the house. He could have been in the can or something, but Slidell, ever careful, imagined

Farley Tanner behind a shotgun aimed right at his head. A Kevlar vest wasn't much good for a head shot, so Slidell decided the better part of valor was to get the hell outta there.

Safely behind his black-and-white, he used his bullhorn. "Farley Tanner. This is the sheriff. Come out with your hands up." As he said it, he noted a crowd beginning to form on the periphery of the squad cars, and thought the announcement sounded a bit theatrical. However, he couldn't think of anything else to say while he was making demands through a bullhorn.

As they waited, tension began to build, especially with the crowd. Someone, probably one of Farley's disciples, began to harangue the officers with shouts of "Waco revisited" and "Storm troopers go home." Still, there was no movement or sound from the house. Now it was time to act. Delay would only make matters worse with the crowd, and surely by now the local media hounds had the scent. Fortunately, Slidell had prepared his men for this contingency, and on his signal, they advanced.

Again Slidell moved to the front door; this time considerably faster and accompanied by Deputy Thomas, "Burley" by nickname, whose hobby for most of his life had been weightlifting. It was Deputy Thomas's job to take the door out. Deputy Thomas enjoyed this type of duty so much, he neglected to check whether the door was unlocked. As it turned out, it wasn't.

Slidell moved directly through the shattered door, followed by six members of the SWAT team. Each man peeled off into different rooms as they made their way down the long hallway, typical of that housing *genre*. It was Slidell's self-appointed duty to secure the room at the end of the hallway, probably the kitchen, the one with the light on.

For those familiar with television drug raids, it isn't that way in reality. The noise produced by the running, door slamming, and screaming makes the whole situation seem like pandemonium. To some extent, with the adrenaline pumping, it is. Many officers have little memory of the raid after the fact.

Slidell, covered with sweat and pistol at ready, reached the back room. It was, in fact, a kitchen with the light on. The remainder of the house secured, a tense silence momentarily cloaked the scene.

"Tanner, if you've got a weapon, throw it out. I don't want to kill you, but I will. I mean it," screamed Slidell. In the midst of the chaos, he had forgotten to identify himself.

Silence.

Taking a deep breath, Slidell swung around the doorsill, weapon pointed, heart pounding.

His first thought was relief. Apparently no one was home. His next thought was the smashed front door – someone would have to answer for that

Then he saw a foot behind the counter. Again the adrenaline pumped.

"Goddammit, Tanner. Come outta there or you're a dead man."

Silence.

Again Slidell charged into the fray, and a less disciplined man would have put a bullet in the corpse.

There was no question. It was Farley Tanner with a neat round bullet hole right in his forehead. Slidell knew he was wasting his time, but he checked Tanner's pulse: deader'n hell. Quickly he gave the "stand down" order before a nervous trigger finger caused more problems.

*****

Joe Don Ling was not a happy camper as he finished up his investigation of the crime scene. Joe Don had been at one of his kid's birthday party when he got the call, and now midnight was becoming a thing of the past.

"Well, Joe Don, whadaya think?" asked Sheriff Goodbee.

"Just what it looks like, Slidell," the coroner answered, in a manner suggesting there was really no need to drag him out at night. Joe Don knew better, but he was entitled to bitch if it made him feel better. "One shot in the forehead at fairly close range. Can't find an exit wound, and because of the size of the entry wound, I'd say it was a small caliber weapon. Probably a twenty-two. Maybe a 'dum dum.' Been dead maybe six, seven hours. Death was instantaneous. You guys find a weapon?"

Slidell shook his head.

They'd take a closer look at the immediate area after the forensics guy finished dusting for prints, but if it was a suicide, the gun would have been fairly easy to find, and it wasn't.

Usually when a guy shoots himself, Slidell was thinking, he doesn't have time to hide the weapon real good. Besides, suicides don't shoot themselves right in the middle of the forehead. No, it wasn't a suicide, and whoever did it had apparently been just ahead of his people, maybe an hour.

After securing the scene upon the arrival of forensics, Slidell and his deputies had spent most of their time searching the house for the treasure Billy Boy Turman had said was there. Turman had described a floor safe in the bedroom that served as Tanner's office. That had been easy to locate. It was open and empty. No treasure. Nowhere.

Slidell was the last to leave the scene. He posted a deputy to keep out intruders, then headed for home.

Sleep probably wouldn't happen, but he was dog tired, and a strong drink would help. He'd get a fresh start in the morning. Maybe forensics would come up with something. Otherwise, he was back at square one. The whole damn thing now made less sense than it did when the beach box first blew up. Everybody else was dead – except Ernie and Billy Boy.

Chapter XIX

Slidell Goodbee sat on the porch in back of his condo. He was staring at a moonlit Santa Rosa Sound while he sipped a cold beer. Daphne Fairhope was inside preparing something, Slidell wasn't sure what, for dinner. He had escaped cookout duty as a byproduct of his mood ever since the Farley Tanner thing. It was a beautiful, uncharacteristically cool night, and there was a lovely and compliant woman just through the door, but Slidell's mind was stuck fast in the mystery of who killed Farley Tanner.

Billy Boy Turman was tucked safely in jail when the murder occurred. Ernie Brown, suspect *numero uno*, had a good alibi: he was sitting at his beach box trying hard to hustle some visiting talent. This was verified by several people, mostly guys who were trying to make a move that Ernie kept blocking, and the talent herself. This contest, which apparently had no winners, went on until sundown, when the lady packed up her stuff and left her suitors to play with each other. By that time, Tanner was a dead guy. Also, although forensics found a ton of fingerprints, none of them were Ernie's.

All the bodies, even what was left of Scudder VanAlstine, had been recovered, and now Billy Boy Turman was looking at multiple indictments, both state and federal. Billy Boy probably wouldn't see Ol' Sparky, but he'd be an old man when he got out of prison. Slidell needed to talk to the respective prosecuting agencies about that.

That left… nobody. A random killer, or even a friend or disciple, wouldn't have known about the treasure. According to Turman, nobody knew but him, Tanner, Ernie, and the dead guys. Of course, maybe Turman didn't know everything, or he was lying. But why lie? An accomplice? Someone who would hold on to the treasure until Turman got out? Not very damn likely. If Turman knew something that he could trade to the law for less time, he'd be on it in a two-count.

So, what? Someone just happened on Tanner while he sat counting his treasure, killed him and took the treasure? Maybe. But why would Tanner be sitting in his meeting house, where anybody could walk through, counting his treasure? Not likely.

A random hijack? A "give me all your money and jewelry" kind of thing? Tanner gave him the treasure, and the guy killed him anyway? Not good odds on that one for a lot of reasons. But stranger things had happened.

If the treasure starts turning up in bits and pieces, we'll move that one to "more likely," thought Goodbee.

The only thing that made any sense was that there was somebody else. Somebody Turman didn't know about. Somebody who knew the operation. Somebody who knew it was all fixin' to come to a screeching halt.

Who might have that last bit of information? Slidell pondered. *My deputies might. But they didn't know until I brought Turman in, and then the only ones who knew what was about to happen were locked up in a conference with me until minutes before the raid. Nobody else knew.*

His head began to spin, and he considered hitting the wall next to him.

As he looked around for something to take his frustration out on, he realized that Daphne was standing behind him, a look of concern on her face.

"Honey," she said sympathetically, "what's wrong? Can I help?"

"No, I'm just trying to wrap up something down at the beach," he said, almost automatically. And then the words seemed to ring in his head, accompanied by a feeling of *déjà vu*. For a moment, their eyes locked.

"Well, if you say so," Daphne recovered. "But come in.

Dinner's ready."

After dinner, Slidell still didn't know what Daphne had prepared. They had said little; Slidell's thoughts had no relation to the meal in front of him. He helped with the dishwashing, and then they retired to the back porch with a glass of wine.

Sitting in silence for some time, Slidell finally turned toward Daphne. "You're the silent partner, aren't you?"

After a shocked pause, Daphne replied, "Why, whatever in the world are you talking about?"

"Sugar, I think you know," answered Slidell. "Mark Albright wasn't at Fairbreeze that night to get in your pants, at least that wasn't his primary assignment. He was Farley Tanner's boy, and Farley ordered him to take you out. You were the silent partner in Tanner's treasure hunt. The money man, generically speaking, of course. Tanner had what he wanted, and didn't want to split it with you.

"It didn't take you too long to figure out why Albright was there, but you couldn't make your move immediately. Besides that, why rush out and stop the treasure flow? Very clever. Very cold.

"Then I inadvertently tipped you that the hunt was about to wrap up. You must have figured that Turman would fold. So you moved quickly. Took out Tanner, and scooped up the treasure. You've got the treasure. Everybody else is dead, and you're home free. Does that sound about right, Daphne?"

Daphne could affect many poses, but she couldn't control her eyes. The one fatal flaw in an otherwise superb sociopath. Slidell knew it, and Daphne knew he knew it. Her eyes had said it. At first defiant, now devious. Finally, frank.

"Guess you're a better cop than I thought. Guess you've figured it out, and got your man, generically speaking," she mocked. "What now, Sheriff? Book 'em, Danno – Murder One?"

Slidell was a good cop, but not that good. He hadn't really thought that far ahead. There wasn't any question of what he was supposed to do, but this was the woman he loved. Blind justice versus… what? A woman who loved him? A comfortable life? The only life he wanted?

For sure she'd get the chair, as an accomplice to all those murders in furtherance of theft, plus the premeditated murder of Tanner.

On the other hand, all the dead guys, except the lieutenant and the Texas tourists, probably wouldn't be missed by anybody, especially the civilized population.

A long moment passed as they looked deeply into each other's eyes.

"I don't know what now," whispered Slidell at length. "I do know that I need to do some thinking. I'll be back later," he said as he walked back through the house toward his squad car.

"I'll be here when you come back," replied Daphne.

He didn't doubt that.

Epilogue

ERNIE "HONEST ERNEST" BROWN continued as a beach vendor, gradually expanding his business to include all of Pensacola Beach and part of Navarre Beach. He now employs twenty full- and part-time people, and spends most of his time supervising his operation and hustling tourists at Casino Beach. An otherwise shoestring operation received a mysterious infusion of cash the year after Farley Tanner was murdered, with a note signed by Kwai Chang Caine.

WILLIAM "BILLY BOY" TURMAN is currently a resident of the Florida Department of Corrections, Starke Unit. He entered a guilty plea to eight counts of murder, one count of arson, two counts of manslaughter, and a single count of conspiracy to steal state treasures. The State Bar of Florida revoked the law license of William Turman. The U. S. Government declined to prosecute. The state sentences will run concurrently, which means Billy Boy will be up for parole after serving fifteen years. In prison, he has developed many relationships, and acts as a "jailhouse lawyer" for death penalty cases.

SHERIFF SLIDELL GOODBEE continues to serve as Sheriff of Escambia County. He is married to Daphne Fairhope Goodbee, and has two children, a boy and a girl. The Goodbees are locally renowned for their many philanthropic contributions, and Slidell Goodbee is considering running for the Senate of the United States.

DAPHNE FAIRHOPE GOODBEE is married with two children. In addition to homemaking and charity work, she is applying for admission to law school. She intends to specialize in criminal law.

THE FAMILIES OF LIEUTENANT RUDOLPH COMMINS AND OF THE TWO INNOCENT BYSTANDERS FROM TEXAS have received anonymous blind trusts to allow for their support and to establish scholarships should their children choose to attend college.

FARLEY TANNER, PERCY MERIWEATHER "SCUDDER" VANALSTINE, MARK ALBRIGHT, AND THE WET TEAM are, as of this writing, all still dead.

JANIE JORDAN (a.k.a. Kimberly Carter) vanished. When law enforcement authorities located her beach house, across from the Surf's Up Tower, the only thing missing was Jordan/Carter. There was nothing traceable – as if the person occupying the residence never really existed.